The Witness in the Window

A noise in the night,
a glance out the window,
a giant step into the world of
adventure and suspense

Agape **Jack Coleman**

Jack Coleman

This book is a work of fiction. Names, characters, places, and incidents are the product of the author's imagination or are used fictitiously. Any resemblance to actual events, locals, or persons, living or dead, is coincidental.

ISBN: 1489558721
ISBN 13: 9781489558725

Library of Congress Control Number: 2013909822
CreateSpace Independent Publishing Platform
North Charleston, South Carolina

To Jean,
God's special gift to me.

She is my faithful companion,
my partner in ministry,
my proofreader and editor
and the love of my life.
Without her encouragement
this book could not have been written.

TABLE OF CONTENTS

CHAPTER 1

The Beginning of Summer

My name is Charlie. Well, actually my name is Charles, but everyone just calls me Charlie. I was born and raised in the sleepy little town of Lee's Junction, Virginia which is nestled in the foothills of the northwestern part of the state. It's not a very big town, but it is the county seat of Stuart County. The county is named after General Jeb Stuart, who was a Confederate Army officer of some note, so I guess that makes it a pretty important place. My folks moved to Lee's Junction from West Virginia when my dad bought the lease on the Esso Station at the corner of Jefferson Davis Avenue and Lee Street. The following year my brother, Bobby, was born and then I came along a couple of years later.

When my dad first opened the station, he mainly just pumped gas and changed oil for the people in town. But later, as he gained experience in the automotive trade, he began to do more complicated engine work. By the time I was six or seven, Dad was known as the best auto mechanic in the whole area and his business really began to prosper.

My mother was a housewife and the best mother in the world. At least I certainly thought she was. She kept our house spick and span and always had some cookies and a big glass of milk waiting for Bobby and me when we got home from school. I probably should tell you that my mom was always hugging and kissing me and calling me her special little man. She had a pet name for my brother too. Bobbikins! Our mother was just that kind of cuddly mother, but I guess it was okay as long as no one was around to see her when she acted like that.

Our family was Presbyterian and we attended Lee's Junction Presbyterian Church where my dad was a deacon and my mom taught the Sunday school class for fourth grade girls. Going to church was all right, but I really preferred Sunday school where we had a lot more freedom. There we could talk and color in our Bible coloring books, but in church we had to sit up straight and at least pretend to be listening. We certainly couldn't sleep in church. If Mom or Dad didn't catch us dozing off, one of the deacons was sure to come down the aisle and prod us awake. That was really embarrassing.

The summer of my eighth year was a memorable one. Having just finished second grade and being officially considered a third grader, I felt as though I had accomplished a major goal in life. But then, I was only eight years old and little steps along the path of life at that age can seem like mighty big achievements. I was looking forward to summer vacation when I could play all day with my buddies. We had a lot planned for the next couple of months, but forthcoming events would soon change all that.

It was a warm day in early June of 1941 when my mother informed my brother and me during breakfast that she and dad were going to drive over to Charlottesville to attend a meeting. Arrangements had been made for us to spend the night with their friends the Franks, and that sounded good to me because I really liked their thirteen year old son, Fred. Plus Mrs. Franks had a reputation for baking the best pies and cakes in town. She also sold tickets at the movie theater on weekends and sometimes had given me a free ticket. It was worth a night away from my own bed to have a slice of her angel food cake and maybe even another free ticket.

Later that same morning my father sat down with Bobby and me on the front porch and had a talk with us about what had happened in town the previous day. He explained that three colored boys had been arrested and were now locked up in the county jail which was right across from where the Franks lived on Court Street. According to my dad, these boys had attacked a young lady as she was taking a shortcut through some woods near the house where we used to live on the other side of town.

It sounded pretty exciting to me. "Did they rob her or what?" I asked.

"No, son. They actually attacked her," my dad replied.

"What does that mean? Attacked her? Did they beat her up or something? I don't understand what happened." I was trying hard to figure out exactly what those boys had done to the lady.

"Well, it's hard to explain to you right now. They did a terrible thing to her which you'll understand about when you get a little older," Dad said.

"I already heard all about it," Bobby told us. "They said she was running down the middle of the main road with all her clothes practically torn off."

My dad interrupted him. "Enough about that, Bobby. Anyway, Chief Dinkins and the State Police were called and I understand that they found the three boys hiding back in the woods and they were falling down drunk."

"What's going to happen to them now?" I asked seeking more details.

"I expect that they'll be brought before a judge who will hold them over for trial at some later date. In the meantime, they have all three locked up in the county jail," Dad replied.

"What about the girl? Is she okay?"

"She's certainly going to live, but those boys did a horrible thing to her and will have to pay dearly for their crime."

Dad started to get up, but I still had more questions.

"Where is she now? Is she in the hospital?"

"I believe they took her to the hospital in Staunton and will probably keep her there for a few days for observation," my dad patiently responded.

"Do we know her?" Bobby asked.

"I don't, but you may have heard of her," Dad answered. "She lives on Lee Street near the school. I don't know her first name, but her family name is Falkner. She works as a waitress at the Midway Restaurant and may have even waited on us when we've had dinner there on a Sunday after church."

I tried to remember, but drew a complete blank. "I don't think I know her, but maybe I've seen her around," I replied.

My dad stood up and I knew that our conversation was coming to a close. "Boys, I think you should stay away from the area around the jail and courthouse for a day or two until this thing cools down. Some of the rabble rousers around town are talking as though they might take the law into their own hands." Giving me a pat on the shoulder, he added, "I know that you are going to be spending the night right across the street from the jail tonight, but Mr. Franks will keep you and Bobby safe. You just mind him and do what he says."

I could hardly wait to get together with some of my friends and talk about this information that I had just been given. Maybe they would know what those guys had actually done to the Falkner girl. I quickly phoned Billy Hanson and arranged to meet with him and the twins, Matthew and Mark Gillman, under the big pine trees across from the park on Lee Street. I was there in five minutes and Billy and the others arrived just a short time later out of breath. They had run all the way.

Each of us had heard different details about the attack on the Falkner girl and each of us had probably embellished them quite a bit. Billy said that he had heard that the girl was Frances Falkner, but that most people called her Fran. Mark told us that he actually knew her and that she was about twenty years old. Matthew piped in and added that she was a cute blonde with a big rear end that jiggled when she walked.

Then Billy informed us that his dad had been downtown and had seen a group of guys standing on the corner by the Rexall Drug Store talking about the incident and sounding pretty worked up about the whole thing. Billy had been warned by his father to stay away from Main Street and also away from the jail because there just might be trouble.

"Does anyone know what rape means?" Billy asked. "My dad said those guys raped her."

Matthew, who seemed to be our authority on things to do with girls, said, "That's when a guy forces a girl to do something that she really doesn't want to do. He makes her do it."

"Yeah, great! But what does that mean?" Billy wasn't going to give up without an answer to his question.

"Come on, grow up! Everyone knows what rape means," Matthew replied, while actually being as uninformed as the rest of us. None of us wanted to sound stupid, so we stopped asking.

"My dad said that he heard that the men over on the corner by the drugstore were talking about lynching the bad guys," Billy added. "But I guess we don't have to worry about that because they've got them locked up tight in the jail."

"If there are enough guys with guns, they could break them out of the jail, just like those bank robbers did in the picture show last Saturday," Mark replied.

"It's lunch time and I'm going to go get a sandwich," Billy said as he stood up to head home. Our meeting was over and we all went our separate ways wondering exactly what it was that had actually happened to Frances Falkner in the woods.

CHAPTER 2

View from the Window

My folks left for Charlottesville that same afternoon after dropping Bobby and me off at the Franks' home. What a great dinner we had! Mrs. Franks fixed hamburgers with all the trimmings, french fries and a giant slice of cherry pie with vanilla ice cream for dessert. When we finished eating, we played "Fish" with Fred on the living room floor as his parents listened to the radio and read the evening paper.

Promptly at nine o'clock Mrs. Franks broke up our card game and told us it was time to turn in for the night. With a minimum of complaint, we all headed to bed. Bobby was to sleep in Fred's room and I was assigned to the small bedroom across the hall on the jail side of the house. As I pulled down the window shade next to my bed, I noticed that I could see the jail right across Court Street. I was really tired and it must have only taken me a few minutes to fall asleep.

Later that night I was suddenly awakened by loud voices coming from the street below my window. I wondered what was going on and quickly I sat up in bed and ducked my head under the window shade to take a look. I could hardly believe what I was seeing.

There were a lot of cars filling the street and a whole bunch of men carrying guns were standing around the jail. The men all had pillowcases with eyeholes cut in them over their heads. I noticed that there were no license plates on any of the cars and the headlights had been turned off, but I could see everything very clearly because of the streetlights.

As I watched, the door of the jail opened and six hooded men came out dragging three naked colored men by their arms. One of colored guys was bleeding pretty badly and they all three looked really scared.

As I knelt there on the bed taking in the scene, one of the men with a gun, who was wearing a black leather jacket with lots of silver studs, leaned over and his hood accidently slipped off. I was able to get a real good look at his face. But just at that exact moment, he glanced up and saw me looking out the window. Before I could even move, he whipped out a flashlight and shined it right in my eyes. I quickly ducked back out from under the window shade and ran out of the room shouting for Mr. Franks.

"Mr. Franks! Mr. Franks!" I yelled as I got into the hallway.

I couldn't believe how fast he emerged from his bedroom. Mr. Franks was just wearing his pajamas and he was followed by his wife who was pulling on a robe over her nightgown.

"What's the matter, Charlie?" he asked. "Did you have a bad dream?"

"No! It's not a dream! There are a lot of men out front in the street who have the colored guys from the jail and they're putting them into their cars right now. Everyone has a gun!" I was so scared that my voice was shaking as I tried to explain to Mr. Franks what was happening.

"Slow down, boy!" he answered. "What are you talking about?"

Just at that moment we heard sound of many vehicles starting up and racing their engines. Mr. Franks ran into my room to see for himself what was going on. Just as he pulled up the shade to look out the window, the cars began driving off.

In less than a minute, he was back into the hall and started asking me questions about what I had seen. "Who were they, Charlie? Did you see their faces? Did you recognize any of the men?"

"They all had pillow cases over their heads, but I knew one of the men," I told him. "His hood slipped off and I saw his face really clearly. But I think that he saw me too. He shined his flashlight right on me while I was there in the window."

"Who was it? Come on, Charlie! Who did you see?" he demanded.

"It was one of the Billows brothers," I replied. "I'm pretty sure that his name is Alvin. He's the one who rides a big red motorcycle with a picture of an Indian chief on the gas tank. I think that he lives down at the end of Church Street near the farms."

"Are you sure that's who it was? Could you possibly be mistaken?" Mr. Franks suggested.

"I don't think so. I see him all the time riding his red bike wearing that black jacket with his name on the back in silver studs. He's always revving his engine trying to impress the girls." I paused for a minute and then added, "He was wearing that same jacket tonight."

By that time, Bobby and Fred had joined us in the hall. Mr. Franks had said that we shouldn't turn the lights on until we were certain that everyone had left the area, so we just stood there in the dark while he checked the street.

Finally the hall light was turned on and Mr. Franks returned. "Everyone seems to have gone and the street is clear, but all the lights in the jail are off. That's pretty unusual because they always leave the outside lights on all night. I better contact the police immediately," he stated as he left to place the phone call.

A few minutes later I could hear him on the phone saying excitedly, "Operator, get me the police and be quick about it! There seems to have been a jailbreak! Hurry! It's an emergency!"

I just stood there in the hall too terrified to move. Mrs. Franks reached out, put her arms around me and assured me that everything was going to be all right. I wasn't sure that I agreed with her, but her hug really felt good and I finally stopped shaking.

It was only a few minutes before we heard police sirens followed by shouting out in the street. A short time later, there was a loud knock at the front door and Mr. Franks went to see who was there while the rest of us cowered in Fred's bedroom. In a few minutes he returned and told us that a policeman was in the living room and wanted to speak to me. Now I was really frightened. I had never actually talked with a policeman before. I would always say hello to Chief Dinkins, the town cop, whenever I saw him on the street, but I had never really, what I would call "talked" to him.

When Mr. Franks and I walked into the living room, I was a little surprised because I actually expected to see Chief Dinkins, but instead there was a state policeman in a fancy grey uniform waiting to see me. I felt kind of silly meeting him in my Lone Ranger pajamas.

Mr. Franks introduced me to the policeman. "This is Charlie Bishop, the boy I was telling you about. He and his brother Bobby are spending the night with us while their parents are in Charlottesville. Charlie is the one who looked out the window and saw what was going on over at the jail."

By this time, I was really scared and I guess it showed because the first thing the officer did was to pat me on the shoulder and tell me not to be afraid. "The bad guys are all gone now, son. There's no reason to be frightened. Why don't you just tell me what you saw? We need all the information you can give us if we're going to catch the men who broke into the jail tonight."

"Well, sir," I stammered, "I heard the noise on the street and it woke me up. I looked out the window and saw a whole bunch of hooded guys with guns out in the street. There were lots of cars there too and none of them had license plates. I noticed that 'cause it seemed kind of funny."

I tried to remember everything that I had seen. "Then six of the men wearing hoods came out of the door dragging three colored boys. They didn't come through the regular jail door over on the side, but they came out from the front door where the jailer and his wife live. The three colored guys didn't have any clothes on and one was bleeding pretty badly from his head. I could see the blood."

The policeman had a lot more questions. "Did you recognize any of the men? What kind of clothes were they wearing? What kind of cars were they driving? And what color were the cars? Tell me everything that you saw. Every little detail is important."

The officer suddenly paused and smiled at me. I think he was trying to get me to relax a little. "Come on, Charlie. Let's sit here on the sofa."

Sitting down next to him, I continued on with my recollection of the night's events. "I was really scared when I saw all those guns and everyone in masks. They were actually just pillowcases, not real masks. Anyway, there was this one guy there and when his pillowcase slipped off, I knew who he was. His name is Alvin Billows. He has three other brothers and I see him all the time wearing his black leather jacket. The jacket has his name "Alvin" in silver studs on the back: A-L-V-I-N. He rides a big red motorcycle that has a picture of an Indian chief on the gas tank. I've never spoken to him but I've seen him riding around lots of times."

"Did you know any of the other men?" the policeman asked. "Can you describe anyone else?"

"No, sir," I replied, trying to sound really respectful. "Like I said, they all had on hoods and I really can't tell one kind of car from another. But I can tell you that there were a lot of cars which all drove off towards Main Street."

The police officer stood up. "You've been a big help, Charlie, and you've been very brave to talk to me in the middle of the night. We may need to talk to you again, so have your father call me just as soon as he gets back in town. I'll leave my card with a number where he can reach me."

Mrs. Franks talked to me for a long time after the policeman left, trying to calm me down and assure me that none of us was in any danger. Finally my eyes began to get heavy and she led me back to bed and tucked me in. I didn't sleep very well that night because I kept dreaming about men wearing hoods and toting guns.

CHAPTER 3

The Only Witness

I woke up really early the morning after the jailbreak, but I didn't get out of bed until I heard others moving about. After getting dressed, I went into the kitchen and found Mrs. Franks already cooking breakfast.

"Well, good morning, Charlie. Were you able to get any sleep after all the excitement of last night?" she asked.

"Not much," I replied. "I kept dreaming about the men who were all wearing hoods and then waking up every hour or so to make sure that they had really gone away."

"It was certainly a pretty scary night and I must admit that I didn't sleep too well either," Mrs. Franks said. "But this is a new day and I'm sure the police have everything well in hand by now," she responded with an encouraging smile.

I hoped that was true because I was still feeling a little shaky. In fact, I didn't have much appetite for breakfast. Mr. Franks, Bobby and Fred ate huge stacks of pancakes, but I just sort of picked at the food on my plate and wondered how much longer it would be until my parents came home.

Mr. Franks seemed to sense that I wasn't feeling very well and tried to cheer me up. "Don't worry, Charlie. It's all over and you'll soon forget all about it. Maybe you boys can go to the movies this afternoon."

Just then the phone rang and Mr. Franks went out in the hall to answer it. Sitting at the kitchen table, we could hear everything that he was saying.

"Yes, this is Mr. Franks. Of course I remember you from last night, Officer. Yes, Charlie is still here, in fact he's eating breakfast right now." Then there was a long pause before Mr. Franks spoke again. "I understand that you need to talk to Charlie again, but I believe it would be best if you waited until his parents return from Charlottesville. They should be back in town by early evening."

Another long pause. "No, he won't be leaving town and he'll be staying right here with us until his folks get back. Charlie's not going anywhere today, except perhaps to the movies later this afternoon. I assume that's all right with you."

The conversation was ending. "Yes, of course. Whatever you think is best. Thank you for calling." We heard Mr. Franks hang up the phone.

"I guess everyone heard what was said," Mr. Franks commented as he came back into the kitchen. "That was the officer who was here last night and he said that the police need to talk with you again, Charlie. I asked that they wait until your mom and dad get home and he said that would be fine. But he did say that you were to stay inside until they arrive back in town."

What a downer. It sounded like I wouldn't be going to the movie after all and it was going to be an all-cartoon show. In fact, it sounded like I couldn't go anywhere at all. It was like I was being punished when I hadn't done anything wrong. I had just been in the wrong place at the wrong time and had seen something that I shouldn't have seen.

14

Mr. Franks sensed my disappointment and said, "Cheer up, Charlie. I'll tell you what I'll do. As soon as I finish this coffee, I'll go into town to the police station and see what I can find out about what happened last night. Then we can begin to make some fun plans for the rest of the day."

We cleared the table and helped Mrs. Franks do the dishes while we waited for Mr. Franks to return. I wondered if the colored boys were still alive or if the hooded men had killed them. Somehow I didn't think there was going to be a happy ending to last night's events.

It was about an hour before Mr. Franks returned and he immediately called the four of us into the living room. Mrs. Franks, Fred, Bobby and I all sat in a circle around him, anxious to hear what he had learned about what had occurred at the jailhouse.

Mr. Franks finally cleared his throat and begin to share with us what the police had related to him. "Some really terrible things took place last night. I figure that you're going to hear it from someone, so you might as well hear it from me. There are going to be a lot of rumors going around about what happened, but this is what the police actually told me."

He leaned forward and started talking to us in almost a whisper. "It seems that it was about two o'clock in the morning when the mob showed up at the jail in their cars. Apparently they banged on the door of the jailer's quarters, the door that opens onto the street. Maybe that's what woke you up, Charlie."

I nodded my head, trying to remember exactly what it was that had brought me up out of a deep sleep. "Maybe, but I'm not sure," I responded.

"Anyway, when the jailer didn't answer quickly enough, they broke through the door, grabbed the jailer and his wife right out of their bed and tied their hands behind them. Then they got the keys to the cells and entered the jail itself. It didn't take them long to find the three colored boys in their cells wearing only their underwear. One of the boys apparently gave them some resistance, so they hit him on the head, probably with one of their guns.

Fred couldn't keep quiet any longer. "This is awful. Did this really happen right across the street?"

"It gets even worse," Mr. Franks stated. "The men actually stripped the boys naked, tied their hands behind them and then six of them dragged the darkies out to where the cars were waiting. The others that were still inside went back into the jailer's quarters and took the jailer and his wife and locked them up in one of the jail cells. I actually don't think that any of the bad guys were in the jail more than a few minutes. Everything happened really fast."

Looking directly at me, Mr. Franks continued. "You apparently saw them bringing out the colored boys and putting them into the cars from the window, Charlie. Well, here's the rest of the story. After they all drove off, they headed west out of town to that big hill about four miles out. You all know the hill I'm talking about?"

In unison, we all nodded our heads, picturing the scene in our minds.

"Maybe you remember that there's a big telephone pole right on the top of the hill and that's where they lynched them. They just hung them all from the cross bar of the pole."

Mr. Franks paused dramatically before adding, "And if that wasn't enough, then they turned their guns on them to make sure that they were really dead and drove away leaving them hanging there. The police found their bodies this morning about daybreak."

We all just sat there. No one said anything. It was almost too horrible to take it all in.

Finally I asked, "So they murdered them and then just left them hanging there? They killed all three of them?"

"Yes, I guess that's about what they did. It's not a pretty story to have to tell you. Who would have ever thought something like this would happen in Lee's Junction?" Mr. Frank put his face in his hands and I even thought for a minute he was going to cry, but instead he looked up and motioned for me to come and sit on his lap.

At eight years old, I felt like maybe I was too big to be sitting on his lap, but I must admit that it felt pretty good. Life had become very complicated all of a sudden.

"It looks like you're the only witness, Charlie," Mr. Franks told me. "So far they haven't been able to find anyone else who saw anything, or at least anyone else who will admit to seeing anything. They're definitely going to want to talk to you as soon as your parents get back. So today you need to stay inside for your own safety until everything is cleared up. Do you understand?"

I really didn't understand why I couldn't go outside, but there was nothing that I could do except nod my head and then lean back against Mr. Franks' shoulder.

The day seemed to drag by. Fred got out his erector set and we built a big crane and that kept us busy for several hours. Then we played every card game that we knew. Finally about five o'clock we started listening to the radio because that's when all the good programs came on. You know the ones I mean: the Green Hornet and the Lone Ranger. Those were my favorites. We hunkered down in front of the radio and gave it our full attention until dinner time. Later Mrs. Franks read us a story until my parents arrived about nine o'clock that night.

What a tale we had to tell them! They had no idea of everything that had taken place in their absence. Dad used the Franks' telephone to call the police and arranged for them to meet with me the next morning at our house. And finally, about an hour later, we went home. I felt much safer with my own family and in my own bed. When Mom came in to kiss me goodnight, I hugged her really, really tight.

I also asked her to leave the bed light on until I went to sleep. It's really scary to be just eight years old and the only witness to a jail break which led to a lynching.

"Goodnight, Charlie," Mom whispered. "Have pleasant dreams."

And I was glad to hear her say that because I really didn't want to dream again about the hooded men and their guns. I was looking forward to a good night's sleep filled with pleasant dreams instead of nightmares.

CHAPTER 4

Police Interrogation

I awoke about six o'clock the next morning, but I didn't get out of bed until I heard Mom and Dad talking in the kitchen over an hour later. Still in my pajamas, I went in to find out what I was supposed to do all day. Dad told me that I should get dressed and eat my breakfast before the police arrived at nine o'clock.

I really didn't have much appetite that morning. I was kind of nervous thinking about talking to another policeman again regarding what had happened. There's something about a policeman in his uniform that's sort of frightening. I can't really explain what it is. Maybe it was the badge.

There was a knock at the front door right as the clock chimed nine o'clock. It wasn't just one policeman, but actually two state policemen and Chief Dinkins. Dad answered the door and invited them into the front room and of course, Mom asked if she could get them a cup of coffee. They said thanks but no thanks and seemed eager to get to the business at hand.

After asking Dad's permission to talk with me, I was called into the room. I was really glad to see that my father was allowed to stay while I was questioned. You can imagine that made me feel a lot better. The policemen were really nice and I wasn't scared at all. They asked me to sit down and then introduced themselves.

"My name is Trooper James," the tall policeman said, "and this is my partner Trooper Jennings. I think you know Chief Dinkins."

I sort of relaxed back into the chair and responded, "Yes, sir. I know the chief and it's good to meet you. Aren't you the one I talked to the other night?"

"That's right," replied Trooper James. "I have several questions to ask you. Some may be the same questions that I asked earlier, but I need you to answer them again just so we can be sure that we have everything right. Don't hurry. Just take your time. We want you to think about your answers and tell us exactly what you saw and heard. Are you ready?"

I took a deep breath. "Yes, sir. I'm ready when you are," I replied.

"First, what's your name?"

That was certainly an easy question. "My name is Charlie Bishop."

"Is that your full name?"

"Well, actually my full name is Charles Edward Bishop, but my folks and my friends call me either Charlie or sometimes Chuck."

"Where were you on the night of June second between midnight and three in the morning?"

I hesitated for a minute. "Was that the day before yesterday?" I asked.

The policeman nodded, so I continued. "I was staying at Mr. and Mrs. Franks' house at the corner of Jackson and Court streets right across from the jailhouse. My brother Bobby and I were spending the night with them because my folks were in Charlottesville at a meeting."

"Where exactly were you sleeping in the Franks' home?"

"Mrs. Franks told me to sleep in the small bedroom across the hall from their room," I told him. "Bobby got to sleep in with Fred in his room because they're pretty good friends. They're almost the same age, you know. Anyway, Fred's room is next to his parents' bedroom."

So far so good. None of the questions were hard to answer.

"Could you see the jail from your room?" Trooper James continued.

Another easy question. "It was right across Court Street."

"Why did you wake up?"

"I heard a lot of shouting and stuff out there on the street."

The questions were coming faster now. "What did you do when you heard all the noise?"

"I just ducked under the shade and looked out the window. You see, the window was beside my bed. All I had to do was sit up in bed and the window was right there." I was finding it a little hard to explain to him.

"So you looked out the window and what did you see?"

Thinking back on what happened, I began to get a little shaky again. "As I ducked under the window shade, I saw a whole bunch of cars parked all around the jail and a lot of guys with pillow cases over their heads. They had holes cut for their eyes so they could see and everybody had a gun."

The words were just tumbling out of my mouth. "There was a lot of shouting, but I couldn't understand what they were saying. I was really scared. It was almost like something from the movies."

"You're doing fine, Charlie," the policeman said. "Just keep going and tell us what you remember."

"Well, this one guy's hood slipped off of his head and I saw his face."

"Did you recognize him? Do you know his name?"

"Like I told you the other night, it was Alvin Billows."

"How do you know it was Alvin Billows?"

I knew that I had told him all of this before, but he seemed to want to hear it all again. "I've seen him lots of times riding his big red motorcycle around town in his black leather jacket. Did I tell you that his name is spelled out on the back of his jacket in silver studs?"

Trooper James didn't say anything. He just nodded his head again, so I kept on talking. "He usually wears an airplane cap. You know the kind with big goggles. Sometimes when he's showing off, he pulls up his goggles and smiles at the girls. He's always trying to get the attention of the girls in town. Everybody knows Alvin and his three brothers."

I stopped for a minute and then said, "Oh, I almost forgot to tell you, his motorcycle is red and has a picture of an Indian chief on the gas tank."

"It must be an Indian motorcycle," the other policeman interjected. I think he was trying to make a joke, but I wasn't sure.

But Trooper James wasn't done with his questions yet. "Have you ever spoken to Alvin Billows? Does he know your name?"

"No, I've never talked to him and I don't think he knows me."

"Do you think he recognized you that night?"

This seemed like a really important question and I thought carefully before I answered. "He did shine his flashlight right on my face and he probably got a good look at me, but I'm not sure. Maybe, but maybe not."

I was ready for the questions to end and I think that the police noticed that I was getting uncomfortable. "You're doing just great, son. I have just a couple more questions and we'll be finished here. What about the cars? Did you recognize any of them?"

"They were just cars like I see every day around town, but there were none that I recognized," I responded wearily.

And then suddenly it was over. "I believe that's all I need to ask today. Thank you, Charlie."

And then turning to my father, Trooper James said, "Mr. Bishop, I do need to talk to you alone for a minute or two. Charlie, you can go into the kitchen with your mom while I tell your dad a few more things."

I was relieved to get out of the chair and stop answering their questions. All I really wanted to do was forget about that night and have things get back to normal. Mom had a glass of milk and some cookies waiting for me on the kitchen table. And she also gave me a big hug and told me not to worry. "It's going to be all right, Charlie. Come on and enjoy your cookies."

A short time later, I heard the front door close and I knew that the policemen had left. Dad's footsteps could be heard coming down the hall toward the kitchen, but as he came through the door, I could see him shaking his head. Somehow I knew by the expression on his face that things weren't going to get back to normal any time soon.

Dad sat down at the table across from Mom and me and gave us the news. "The police want to know if there is some place out of the area where Charlie can safely stay for several days until they get this thing under control. They seem to think that he could be in some danger since the man on the street actually saw his face."

THE WITNESS IN THE WINDOW

My mother looked downright alarmed. "Why does Charlie need to leave home? Surely the police can protect him right here in Lee's Junction."

"Actually, I think the police are right," my dad replied. "If this Billows fellow actually recognized Charlie, he could have told some of the others that were at the jail with him that night. If that's the case, they might try to do something to keep Charlie from testifying against them."

"But where can he go?" Mom asked.

Dad thought for a minute or two and then answered, "How about with your folks in Quinnimont? Charlie loves your mom and dad. And don't forget that Tommy and Dave, your two youngest brothers, are there. Charlie would have a great time with them."

It almost seemed like my dad was getting excited over the thought of sending me away from home.

"Yes," Dad continued, "that could work out just fine. Quinnimont is a really small place tucked away in the hills of West Virginia. No one would think to look for Charlie there and I'm not sure that anyone here in Lee's Junction even knows where your parents live." Then turning to my mother, he asked, "What do you think, Mary Beth?"

Mom thought for a moment and then answered, "Yes. That actually would be a great place for Charlie to spend a week or two. He would have a wonderful time with his uncles. They're always fishing and wandering around in the hills doing this and that."

Then she turned to me and said, "This would be a great adventure for you, Charlie. How about a trip to see Grandpa and Grandma Wilson? Wouldn't you like that?"

"Well, I don't know. I really don't want to leave my buddies here. We've got some big plans alrcady figured out for the summer," I added.

"The plans will keep and your friends will be here when you get back. You'll have a wonderful time in Quinnimont. I know you'll like it there. It will be a big summer adventure," Dad concluded.

So it was quickly settled. I was going to visit my grandparents in Quinnimont, West Virginia, but I wasn't to tell anyone where I was going or even that I was leaving town. The whole thing was to be kept as a big secret.

CHAPTER 5

Quinnimont

We left for Quinnimont early the next morning. Mom had helped me pack my suitcase the night before. I took my jeans and T-shirts and had made sure that I included my swimming trunks and baseball glove. My mother also reminded me that I had to take clothes for Sunday mornings because Grandma and Grandpa never missed going to church.

Dad already had the car gassed up and we were ready to leave by six o'clock. The streets were deserted that early in the morning and we didn't see a single person or even another car as we left Lee's Junction. We had told no one that we were leaving, not even the Franks. Dad had just put up his "Gone Fishing" sign on the gas station door.

Bobby was going along with us, but he would be returning home with Mom and Dad the next day. He had been warned very sternly not to mention to anyone about our trip to Quinnimont or where I was staying. My folks were taking no chances that my location would become known. I wasn't sure how they were going to explain my absence, but that wasn't my problem so I certainly wasn't going to worry about it. Actually, I was beginning to get a little excited about the time I was going to be spending with Grandpa and Grandma and my two uncles.

We drove south on Route 11 to Lexington and then turned west onto Route 60 toward Charleston, West Virginia. I fell asleep as we were crossing North Mountain on the way to Clifton Forge and didn't wake up until we had crossed the border into West Virginia. We stopped for lunch at a place Dad knew in the little town of Sam Black's Church. It looked like a real dump to me, but Dad said it served the best barbecue he had ever tasted. Then we were back on the road again heading south through Meadow Bridge and down the mountain on Highway 41 to Quinnimont.

Quinnimont had been built as a coal-mining town on the banks of New River along Laurel Creek. It really wasn't much of a town. In all of Quinnimont there were only about fifty houses and every house looked pretty much the same. Of course, there was also the company store on the main street where everyone shopped. Dad told me that the miners didn't use "real money" when they shopped. They had to use "miners' script" for their purchases. I thought that was pretty funny. Almost like Monopoly money.

The reason that my grandparents lived where they did was because Grandpa was the yard master for the C&O railroad that hauled all the coal from the area. The mainline passed right by the town and there was a spur line that ran north to several mines owned by the Byron Coal Company near Layland. Being the yard master was a pretty important job because Grandpa controlled the local switching of trains and had charge of the control lights for the rail lines in the whole district. He worked in a small two-story tower-like building connected to other railroad offices by telegraph and telephone. When we had visited my grandpa the year before, he had even let me pull down one of the switches. Of course, Grandpa was watching me very closely to be sure that I did it just right.

In Quinnimont there was also a small railway station where a couple of local trains stopped each day. The fast passenger trains generally passed right on by and the passengers hardly even noticed that they had gone through the town. There was also a two-car passenger train that made a daily trip up the spur line to Layland. My uncle Tommy worked a few hours every day at the station loading and unloading baggage and mail. It wasn't a full time job, but it did give him a few dollars each week.

You're probably wondering why the town was named Quinnimont. Grandpa told me that the name came from French trappers who had come through there in the olden days. They had called the place Quinnimont because of the five mountains that surrounded the area. It was really a beautiful spot right on the big bend in New River, but most folks passed it by without a thought. State Highway 41 ran along the mountain to the northwest, but it was several hundred feet above the floor of the valley where the village was located. From the highway, one had to look quickly to even see the small town nestled there between the mountains.

The closer to Quinnimont we got, the more excited I became about being with my grandparents and two young uncles. Grandpa and Grandma actually had raised seven boys, but five of them were grown and married with families of their own. Only Tommy and Dave were still at home. That was probably a good thing since there were only three bedrooms in their small company house.

It was "hugging and kissing time" when we finally arrived in Quinnimont. Grandma had dinner ready and waiting for us and she is probably one of the best cooks in the whole world. I was so tired that I almost fell asleep at the table while the grownups were talking over their coffee. I'm not sure why I was tired because I had slept practically the whole time in the car. Maybe it was just all of the excitement of the past few days. Everything had happened so fast.

When we finally all bedded down for the night, I was glad that I had dozed off during the long ride to Quinnimont. With eight of us sleeping in the small house, Bobby and I ended up stretched out on mats on the living room floor. It was kind of fun, but I was glad that it was only for one night. Mom told me that I should just pretend that I was camping out.

The next morning shortly after breakfast, my folks and Bobby left for the long ride back home. I can remember standing at the front gate waving as they drove off with my cheeks still damp from Mom's kisses. I was thinking of the good time I was going to have, but I was still a bit sad as I watched the car drive off. I had never really been separated from my whole family before, but somehow I knew that it was going to be an exciting couple of weeks there in Quinnimont.

Grandpa put his arm around my shoulder as we stood there together by the front gate. "Come on, Charlie. Let's go back in the house. Your summer adventure is about to begin."

Truer words have never been spoken.

CHAPTER 6

Gone Fishing

My mother once told me that my grandpa wasn't just smart, but also very wise. When I asked her the difference, she remarked that I could compare Grandpa to a wise old owl.

"An owl has such good eyesight that it can spot things that other birds can't even see," she informed me. "Your grandfather is very much like that. He has an amazing amount of knowledge about a lot of things. Instead of a wise old owl, your grandpa's a wise old man," she said with a smile on her face. "Sometimes I think he knows too much."

And it was true. My grandfather knew just about everything there was to know and I loved to spend time with him. He had lots of stories about when he was young and was always telling jokes that made me laugh. I thought he must be the best grandpa in the whole world.

The first afternoon that I was in Quinnimont, Grandpa came home from work early and asked if I wanted to go with him for a walk. My grandfather didn't walk very fast because he had bad feet and used a cane. I think he had diabetes or something like that. Anyway, because of the problem with his feet, he had to give up his job as a conductor on the railroad and became the yardmaster instead. He said that was a good thing because he liked being a yardmaster a lot better.

Grandpa had been born in the hills of West Virginia near the Tug and Big Sandy rivers in Mingo County. His folks died in a flu epidemic when he was about my age and he was raised by family friends. He once told me that he knew some of the Hatfield boys, the same Hatfields who feuded with the McCoy clan from across the river in Kentucky. He may have just been telling me one of his yarns (for which he was famous), but I'm not really sure. It might have been a true story. You just never knew with Grandpa.

As a young man, my grandpa had been in the army and served in the Spanish American War and also World War I. He often told me stories about being with Teddy Roosevelt's Rough Riders in their charge up San Juan Hill.

But when I tried to talk to Grandma about this remarkable experience that Grandpa had related, she just laughed and told me that he had actually been a cook and certainly was not part of the Rough Riders. It was hard to know which story to believe. But it didn't really matter to me because I loved all his exciting yarns. And thinking about it, Grandpa was actually a pretty good cook and liked to help Grandma in the kitchen. He made really great pancakes, so maybe he had been a cook back then. I decided not to ask him any more questions about the Rough Riders.

My walk with Grandpa the second day I was in Quinnimont was really special. I felt so happy following in Grandpa's foot-steps and the whole time I didn't trip on a rock or fall over a branch. Sometimes I was pretty clumsy, so my mother had always told me to be careful and to keep my eyes on the path ahead. As we walked along Laurel Creek, which flowed just a few yards east of the house, I felt really safe. I almost forgot about what had happened at the jail just a few days before and that I was actually "hiding out" in Quinnimont.

Suddenly Grandpa stopped and said, "Here we are, Charlie. This is my special fishing hole. What do you think? How would you like to do some fishing?"

I looked around me with surprise. The path had led us into a glen at the foot of the mountain. The little creek had spread out and formed a small crystal-clear pool. It was like a little hideaway there in the valley, almost like something out of a fairy tale book. Ringing one side of the pool were split logs that served as benches.

"Golly, Grandpa," I replied. "This is great. But you forgot to bring the fishing poles with us."

"Where's your faith, boy?" he replied with a smile. "You don't need any store-bought pole to go fishing. You've been living in the city too long."

Then he turned and pointed his long skinny finger toward the nearby woods, handed me his pocket knife and told me to go and cut off two long thin branches to serve as our poles. "You'll know them when you see them," he instructed me. "Smooth and straight. That's the formula. Just pull off all the leaves."

I felt like I was on a treasure hunt as I searched among the bushes and trees for the absolutely perfect branches that would become our fishing poles. I didn't want to disappoint Grandpa with any second-class sticks that didn't measure up to his expectations.

Then I saw the two low branches right next to each other near the base of a tall tree. It was like they were just there waiting for me to come along and cut them off. I knew that my grandpa couldn't help but be pleased with these two beauties.

"Hey," I shouted, "I found them. Look, I've got two of them." Running back to the glen, I presented them to Grandpa and I could tell by the big smile on his face that he liked them too.

Making a feeble joke, I said, "What are we going to do with these poles now? Hit the fish over the head with them?" But suddenly it was like Grandpa turned into a master magician. He reached deep into the pocket of his trousers and took out a small ball of string. And then before you could say "hocus-pocus", he whipped some safety pins out of his shirt pocket. What an amazing grandfather I had!

As I watched, he quickly tied the string to the small end of the stick and then the open safety pin to the end of the string. "Fish hooks really work best, but we don't happen to have any right now. These pins will work just as well as the fancy hooks that cost six for a dime at the company store."

I may not have been a fisherman, but even I knew that the fish weren't going to bite on an old pin like that. We were going to need some bait to catch a fish. "Do you have the bait in your other pocket?" I asked.

"Nope. You're going to have to supply the bait today. Why don't you go over there by the creek and turn over a few rocks and see if you can't find a worm or two or maybe even a cricket. Fish love worms and crickets and I suspect the fish out there are getting mighty hungry about now."

Grandpa pulled out his pocket watch and looked at it closely. "Yep, it's definitely their dinner time, so go rustle up some juicy worms for them and let's entice those fish with something they'll really like."

It only took me about two or three minutes to uncover some of the best looking worms I had ever seen in my whole life. It was like those worms were just waiting there for me to come along and capture them. This was what real fishing was all about.

And when we dropped those baited pins into the water, the fish came swarming around them. I was amazed. There were some really big fish and they were almost fighting each other for the worms.

"I guess we're going to catch a hundred fish today," I exclaimed. "Won't Grandma be happy when she sees us bringing dinner home?"

"Well," Grandpa answered, "we can probably talk your grandmother into frying up a few for us when we get back to the house. Let's see how many we catch first. If we're able to pull in a lot, we can throw the small ones back to catch another day. This is really just sort of a practice fishing time for you."

In a way, I was happy that we were going to let some of the fish go free. While I was there by the pond, I had started thinking again about the bad men who the police said wanted to catch me because I saw them drag off those colored boys. I guess I needed to be very careful and stay close to my grandpa in case those guys ever decided to start "fishing" for me.

Catching fish turned out to be really easy and when we had put aside about ten of the biggest sunfish, Grandpa showed me how to string them on a stick. I can tell you that I was one proud little boy carrying our catch back up the path to the house.

"We're not quite done with the fish yet, Charlie," Grandpa said. "We have to gut them now and clean away their scales. Then we can turn them over to your grandma to fry for us."

I watched carefully as Grandpa gutted the first fish. I felt really sorry for the fish as it certainly wasn't a very pleasant sight to see what was happening to it. In a way it made me think of poor Frances Falkner again and how they said she ran down Main Street naked after being attacked.

These bad thoughts kept coming back to me on and off. I may have left Lee's Junction, but I obviously had brought some of the memories of what happened when I was at the Franks' house along with me to Quinnimont.

But I forgot about the bad memories when I got around to eating the fish. They were definitely the best fish I had ever eaten in my whole life.

CHAPTER 7

Good Church People

I soon learned that spending time at my grandparents' house also meant spending a lot of time at the church. They were definitely church going people. Whenever the church door was opened, they were there. In fact, they were usually the first ones inside the door. Grandpa and Grandma loved the Lord.

The church was a small white frame building located on the main road right at the top of the hill. There was a small belfry on the roof with a bell that someone rang whenever it was time for a church meeting. My grandpa had promised me that if I was quiet during church, he would make arrangements for me to actually ring the bell sometime.

Grandpa was one of the deacons and was responsible for all offerings that were received. That was a pretty important job to be in charge of all the money. But even more important than counting the money and taking it to the bank was that sometimes when the pastor wasn't in town, my granddad got to preach the sermon and lead the singing. He did much better with the preaching than with the singing. Sometimes when Grandpa would sing, it wouldn't sound like the same tune the organist was playing, but at least he was loud and everyone could hear him.

Uncle Dave had an important job in the church too. He was the one who pumped the organ from the room that was behind the pulpit. The old organ at the church was powered by a bellows which had to be pumped by hand in order for the organ to function. During choir practice on Friday evening, I had gone to the church with my uncle and watched him pumping away on the bellows while Mrs. Murdock was playing the organ. It looked like pretty hard work to me, having to standing up the whole time and move the handle up and down. I noticed that Uncle Dave was sweating and I hoped that when I got to ring the church bell it would be easier than pumping the bellows.

Everyone seemed to really like the pastor, Reverend Samuel Smalls, but he didn't live in Quinnimont and usually only came to preach about once a month. I was told that he had the oversight of several other small churches in neighboring towns. I think he was what they call a circuit preacher.

The second Sunday that I was with my grandparents, Grandma told me that after church we were all going down to the river to watch some people get baptized. I couldn't imagine why we had to go to the river because back home in Lee's Junction, they did that right in the church on almost any Sunday morning. The parents would bring their baby up to the front and then the pastor would sprinkle its head with a handful of water from a silver bowl. I tried to explain to my grandma how we did it in the Presbyterian Church.

But Grandma just laughed. "That's not real baptism," she explained. "That's just when they 'christen' a baby. The word 'baptism' means to put someone completely under the water."

I was actually thinking that you could drown a little baby that way and I must have looked a little confused because Grandma added, "You can't baptize babies, you can only dedicate them to the Lord. You have to be old enough to understand that you are a sinner and need Jesus as your Savior to be baptized."

"No one ever told me that," I replied. "Where did you learn so much about God and the Bible?"

"I guess you could say that I learned it at my mother's knee," she told me. "Mother would read the Bible to us children every night before we went to bed and if we didn't understand something, we could always stop her and ask her what it meant."

Grandma paused for a moment and then asked, "Doesn't your mother ever read the Bible to you and Bobby?"

I couldn't remember my mother ever reading the Bible to my brother and me. I had seen her reading it a couple of times and I knew she kept a Bible on her bed table, but I had never heard anyone reading anything out of the Bible except at church.

What could I say? "No ma'am, I guess not."

Grandma had another question. "Do you say your prayers at night when you go to bed, Charlie?"

I just sort of hung my head and replied, "Sometimes."

Just then Uncle Dave walked into the room and my conversation with Grandma came to an end before I had a chance to tell her that I had been praying a lot since the night the men broke into the jailhouse. I was really hoping that God was hearing my prayers and would keep me safe.

Chapter 8

Down By the Riverside

Later that afternoon we all met at the church to go down to the river. No one was dressed for fishing or swimming. There were no overalls or swimming suits. No way! Everyone was all dressed up in their Sunday best and carrying their Bibles. The men all had on neckties for the important event and the ladies had on really nice dresses. You could tell that this was some kind of special occasion.

I walked along with Grandma, Grandpa and my uncles, following the other church members right through the main part of town. We passed the company store and the ball field and finally crossed over the railroad tracks near the station. There was a well-worn path through the brush the led down to the swimming hole. Someone began to sing a hymn just about the time we got to the tracks and everyone kept on singing as we walked along together.

As we neared the river, I could see that there were three men and a lady already there awaiting our arrival. They weren't all dressed up in fancy clothes like the rest of us and I even noticed they had bare feet.

I didn't recognize any of them and I asked Grandpa who they were. He replied that they were "the candidates" for baptism. I had heard the word "candidate" before, but I thought it only referred to someone running in an election. I was soon to learn that in church it had a completely different meaning.

The pastor was also standing there by the river and he wasn't dressed in his church clothes either. I figured he must have gone home and changed when the service was over. Oh, he was still wearing a suit, but it looked a bit worn and you could see the fraying at the sleeves and the bottoms of his trousers. However, he was carrying the same big black Bible that he read from at church and looked pretty impressive to me.

Once everyone had gathered at the side of the river, the pastor opened his Bible and began to read about how Jesus had been baptized in the River Jordan. Then everyone sang another hymn. I didn't know the words so I just pretended to sing along with everyone else.

As the last note died down, the pastor held up his hand. I guess that was so that no one started another hymn. Everyone in the church seemed to really enjoy singing together, but finally it was quiet.

"Are the candidates for baptism all here?" the pastor asked.

The four people standing off by themselves all raised their hands and when the pastor motioned to them to come closer, they quickly walked over to stand facing him at the water's edge.

Pastor Smalls addressed the young woman first. "Sheila, why are you here with us today?"

Looking very solemn, she replied, "I'm here to be baptized."

"Why should I take you into these waters?"

"Well, Pastor, I think everyone in town knows all about me. Ain't no secret that I've been living with Stretch for a couple of months, but now I done moved back home with my folks and made peace with God. Last week I asked Jesus to forgive me and I know that He has. I told the Lord right there and then that I would ask for baptism the next time you took folks to the water, so here I am. I need to be baptized."

There was a big smile on the pastor's face as he replied, "That's a good confession and I know that it pleased the Lord. Now I can take you into the water."

Pastor Smalls then handed his Bible to my grandfather and led Sheila out into the river until they were about waist deep in the water. Laying his hand upon her head, he prayed over her. I couldn't hear the words because he was praying very softly, but I'm sure that the Lord heard every word.

Everything happened really fast then. The pastor told Sheila to hold her nose and close her mouth, and then taking her free hand in his and putting his other hand behind her back, he said in a loud voice, "I now baptize you in the name of the Father, the Son and the Holy Ghost!" With that he lowered her backward into the water until you couldn't even see her anymore and then raised her up again.

Sheila came out of the water soaking wet with a big smile on her face. "Praise the Lord! Hallelujah! Hallelujah!" she was shouting.

And everyone on the shore was shouting and clapping. I realized that I was shouting too. Baptism was certainly an exciting time. It was a lot more exciting than watching a baby get sprinkled with a little water.

Sheila waded back to the riverbank and a lady who was waiting there put a big towel around her shoulders and gave her a hug.

Then the pastor called out, "Who's next?"

"I guess that's me, Preacher," responded a tall lanky young man as he stepped forward.

What's your name, son?"

"Folks all call me Stretch, but my real name is Samuel Kyle Merson."

"Well, Samuel Kyle Merson, why should I take you into the waters of baptism today?"

I had to strain to hear what Stretch was saying, but I when I listened carefully, I could hear every word very clearly.

"Pastor, I'm the one who caused Sheila to sin. She was a good girl until she met up with the likes of me. I almost forced her to come and live with me and share my bed. But I knowed what we were doing was wrong and I had no peace. Finally one night last week, I got down on my knees and asked Jesus to forgive me. After I prayed, it was like a heavy load done been lifted off my back and I felt so clean."

There were tears rolling down the man's cheeks as he continued his confession. "Then I went and asked Sheila to forgive me and we prayed together and gave our hearts to the Lord. She moved out that very same day and now we've both come to be baptized. I done asked Sheila to marry me and she said that she would, so I guess you'll be doing a wedding soon."

"Praise God, Samuel. It sure sounds as though you've gotten yourself saved. Now come on down into the water with me," the pastor invited.

With those words, Samuel (or Stretch as he liked to be called), waded into the river. The pastor prayed a short prayer as he laid his hand upon Stretch and then lowered him down into the water to baptize him.

The man came back up out of the water shouting in words that I couldn't understand and one of the women cried out, "He's got the Holy Ghost! He's really been set free!"

Again everyone broke into song and it was a time of real celebration. I really didn't understand exactly what was happening, but the people were all shouting and rejoicing there by the river and I was glad to be with them for the baptism. After some more singing, the last two candidates were finally baptized. Each of them gave a testimony (that's what Grandpa said it was called) before being lowered into the water. Finally the pastor asked, "Is there anyone else here who feels the call to come to the waters of baptism?"

It was very quiet and then Grandpa spoke up and in a loud voice asked me, "Charlie, how about you? Are you ready to be baptized?"

Caught by total surprise, I stammered, "Uh-uh, no, sir! I don't think I'm quite ready just yet."

The pastor then addressed my granddad saying, "I think perhaps you should talk to this young man a little more before he makes a big decision like this. Maybe next month he'll be ready to follow the example of the four young people he has seen go to the water today."

I have to admit that I was really relieved to get a reprieve. Reaching over, I took hold of Grandpa's hand and gave it a reassuring squeeze. I didn't want him to think I was mad at him for putting me on the spot like that. And who knows, maybe sometime during the summer I would be ready and willing to go into the river and be baptized.

Pastor Smalls had turned his attention to those gathered on the riverbank and announced, "A few of the ladies have prepared some refreshment in that clearing up the path a bit. Everyone go help yourselves and I'll join you just as soon as I get out of these wet clothes. Be sure to welcome these newly baptized brethren."

With that the baptism was over and everyone adjourned to help themselves to the picnic snacks.

"You know, I was baptized when I was just nine years old," Uncle Dave told me as we walked along the path together, "so you're really not too young to think about getting saved. When you're ready to take that step, tell Grandma or Grandpa and they'll pray with you." He paused and then added, "After all, you don't want to get baptized until you're really sure that you're saved and going to heaven."

It was all pretty confusing. I didn't know what he meant about getting saved, but I knew I was certainly asking God to save me from the wicked men who had lynched the colored guys. I probably really did need to talk to Grandpa and find out what getting saved had to do with baptism.

That sunny day by the river was my introduction to water baptism and small country-church style religion, but I guess what I really needed was an introduction to Jesus as my Savior.

CHAPTER 9

The Letter

I was having a great time in Quinnimont fishing in the creek, paddling around in the river and talking walks with Grandpa. I had been a little homesick in the beginning and I still missed my parents, but now every day seemed to hold a new adventure.

Meanwhile the police had been very busy back in Lee's Junction. Two days after the three colored men were taken from the jail and lynched, several Virginia state policemen arrived in town to begin their investigation of the incident.

Among those in the first group of suspects to be interviewed was Alvin Billows, the man I had recognized from my window the night of the lynching. Apparently the police were being very careful not to even drop a hint that they had a lead as to the identity of anyone in the lynch mob. And they certainly didn't want to point a finger directly at Alvin until they had more evidence.

All of those who were brought in for questioning were asked to make a statement concerning their whereabouts on the night of the incident. Most of them had family and friends who were willing to swear as to their locations on the night in question. The suspects were also interrogated as to what type of gun or guns they owned. Practically everyone in Lee's Junction owned a gun. Maybe not a pistol, but certainly a hunting rifle or shotgun. No one was arrested in the first round of inquiries and the police appeared to be totally stumped.

There had been no fingerprints left at the scene and the jailer and his wife could add nothing that would help to identify any of those who took the Negroes from the county jail. The police continued their investigation, but seemed to be hitting a blank wall.

My parents had been cautioned to keep the fact I was with my grandparents in Quinnimont a secret since I was the only witness who could positively identify any of the lawbreakers. The police pointedly asked them if they had received any mail from me. By that time I had already written them two short letters, but apparently they hadn't yet been delivered. Mom and Dad were told to be very careful that they didn't share the contents of my letters with anyone because they might give a clue as to where I was staying.

What no one knew was that a member of the lynch gang actually worked in the local post office and had been told to watch out for any unusual mail that looked like it might have been written by a youngster and addressed to a family in Lee's Junction.

While Alvin Billows didn't know my name, he did know that there had been a young boy who had seen him from the window of the house across the street from the jail. Alvin had also done some checking around and learned that the people who lived in that house only had one son, a boy who was much older than the kid he had seen in the window. Alvin had a strong suspicion that the young witness had been taken out of town to an unknown location for safekeeping. Alvin may have been stupid, but he wasn't dumb.

THE LETTER

Finally one of my letters arrived in the Lee's Junction post office and the postal worker sorting the mail noticed the boyish printing on the envelope that was addressed to Mr. and Mrs. Bishop. The postmark read "Quinnimont, West Virginia."

"Could this possibly be from the kid in the window that saw Alvin?" he asked himself.

Quickly he got to a telephone and placed a call to the ringleader of the gang that had been responsible for the lynching, a local farmer by the name of Jasper Jenkins. The clerk was nervous because he had been warned to keep his contacts with anyone involved in the jail episode guarded. He was well aware that the telephone operators could recognize everyone in the area by their voices, so he was very careful to disguise his manner of speaking as he asked to be connected to Jasper's number.

"This is Clarence Cogbill from the post office," he said quickly as Jasper answered the phone. "I think I may have a lead on the kid in the window."

"Really? How did you get it?" Jasper asked impatiently.

"A letter came in today's mail addressed to Mr. and Mrs. Bishop. It's obviously written by a child and was posted in Quinnimont, West Virginia, wherever that is," Clarence replied. "I just happen to know that the Bishops have two sons, one about twelve and the other maybe eight or nine. I think their names are Bobby and Charlie."

"Which one of the boys wrote the letter?"

"I'm not sure, but the older boy came by to get their mail yesterday, so the letter must have come from the little one, Charlie."

"What's the name of that place again? Quinnimont, you say?" Jasper asked, eagerly seeking more information.

"That's right, Quinnimont." Clarence glanced down at the envelope he was holding in his hand and slowly spelled out the name of the town for Jasper. "It's in West Virginia, but I really don't know exactly where. It could be located anywhere in the whole state."

"We had best look into this," Jasper said, bringing the conversation to a close. "I'll get hold of some of the guys and get them right onto it. Thanks so much for giving me a call. I appreciate it."

With that, Jasper hung up his phone and pondered who would be the best person to contact about this new information. "Why not put Alvin Billows on it?" he thought. "After all, it was his hood that slipped off that night, so he should really be the one to handle the problem with the kid."

Immediately Jasper picked up the phone again and called the Billow's house, leaving a message that Alvin should come by to see him as soon as he got home.

It was only about an hour later when Jasper heard the sound of Alvin's motorcycle pulling up in front of his house. "Glad you're here, Alvin. Come on in." he called out as he opened the door. "We've got some important business to discuss right now."

"What kind of business?" asked Alvin as he quickly came up the steps and into the house, "What's up?"

"It's about that boy you saw in the window the other night. I think I know what his name is and where we can locate him," Jasper answered.

Alvin's mouth turned up into a sneer. "Oh, yeah? If I ever find him I'm going to shut his mouth for good. What's his name?"

"Now don't be in a hurry," Jasper replied trying to calm Alvin down. "We've got to be sure that it's the right kid. And besides, if my information is correct, he's not even here in Lee's Junction right now."

"Really? Where is he?" Alvin inquired anxiously.

"It looks like he might be in a little town in West Virginia named Quinnimont. Have you ever heard of a place called Quinnimont?"

"Can't rightly say that I have," Alvin replied, "but I'm sure gonna to find out where it is. What's the kid's name anyway?"

"I think it may be Charlie Bishop. He's the youngest son of Rob Bishop, the fellow who runs the gas station over on Jackson Street. You probably have bought gas over there and know him."

You could tell that Alvin was still upset, but he seemed to be calming down a little as their conversation continued. "Sure, I know Rob Bishop. I stop by there all the time. You think it's his kid that seen me?"

"It certainly seems that way," Jasper responded. "Clarence Cogbill, who works at the post office, noticed a letter in today's mail obviously written by a child. The letter was addressed to the Bishops and postmarked from Quinnimont, West Virginia."

Jasper stood to his feet. "When you find out where this place is, let me know and then we can do some asking around. Meanwhile, keep this to yourself. We don't want the wrong people to find out that we're looking for this Bishop kid."

"No problem. Mum's the word," Alvin promised. "I'll get right on this. The sooner we put a lid on things, the better, ain't that right?"

The two men shook hands and their clandestine meeting had come to an end. However, that handshake also marked a beginning of a frantic and desperate search for a boy named Charlie Bishop–the witness in the window.

Chapter 10

Safety First

As soon as Alvin left the Jenkins' house, he went to find a road map of West Virginia. What better place to look than the Bishop's Esso Service Station? They had maps there of all the surrounding states.

When he arrived at the station, he found that Bobby, the older Bishop boy, was minding the station while his dad had gone to the cafe for a cup of coffee and a doughnut.

"Got any maps of West Virginia?" Alvin inquired.

"Sure, right over there in the rack. Help yourself," Bobby replied.

Alvin looked over the rack and found the map he was looking for. "Thanks, see you around," said Alvin as he left the station.

Bobby stood at the door for a minute or two and watched as Alvin got on his motorcycle and rode away. There was something familiar about the biker and he tried to think of who the fellow was. Suddenly it came to him.

"That was Alvin Billows!" he thought. "It has to be him. Look at that leather jacket. He's the guy Charlie said he saw in the street by the jail the night of the lynching. I need to tell Dad about this as soon as he gets back."

When his father returned to the station, Bobby rushed out to meet him. "Dad, guess who came in while you were gone?" he asked.

"The President?" Mr. Bishop joked.

"No, Dad. Be serious. It was Alvin Bishop! You know, the guy Charlie says that he saw that night."

"Are you sure, Bobby? What did he want?"

"He just asked for a map of West Virginia. Then he took one of the maps and left."

"You've got to be kidding," Mr. Bishop exclaimed. "A map of West Virginia? I think that I better get in touch with Trooper Jennings or one of the other policemen right away. I'll be back just as soon as I can. You'll watch the place for me again, won't you?"

With that, Bobby's father rushed out to his car and drove away.

Trooper Jennings wasn't at the station when he arrived, but had left one of the detectives in charge who had come to town for the investigation of the lynching. Although Mr. Bishop had met him a day or so previously, he couldn't recall the officer's name.

Walking up to the desk, he announced, "I'm Rob Bishop. I believe you remember me, don't you?"

"Yes, of course I do," the officer replied, recognizing him immediately. "You're the father of our star witness, aren't you?"

"That's right, and I have something you might be interested in."

Charlie's dad then related how Alvin Billows had just come into his gas station and picked up a free road map of West Virginia.

"I wonder why a local boy would want a free map of West Virginia?" the detective asked.

"I don't know," Mr. Bishop answered, "but it worries me. You probably know that's where we took our son, Charlie, so that he would be in a safe place. Could those men have possibly gotten some information about where he is? We haven't told a soul. Not even our best friends know that Charlie is in Quinnimont with his grandparents."

The detective pondered the situation for a few moments and then said, "We best take a few precautions and advise the folks there in West Virginia to be on the lookout for any strangers coming into the town where your son is staying. Can you get word to your relatives there?"

"I'll do that right away," Rob Bishop replied as he turned to leave the station house. "I appreciate your help."

Realizing that it would take about three days for a letter to reach his wife's family, Mr. Bishop thought that it would be best to try to contact them by phone. He was well aware that the telephone operators were the biggest gossips in town, so he decided not to use a local phone. Instead he drove over to Redbank where he could make the call from a friend's house.

It took several tries before contact was finally made with Charlie's grandfather, Wilbur Wilson. After learning that everything was going well there in Quinnimont, Charlie's dad quickly explained the situation and expressed his concern for the safely of his son.

The two of them decided that the best move would be to have Tommy and Dave take Charlie camping for a few days to get him out of town. Mr. Wilson also agreed to alert the railroad detectives, the only lawmen in the area, to be on the lookout for any strangers nosing around. Quinnimont was so small that any newcomer would stick out like a sore thumb.

After Wilbur once more assured Rob Bishop that Charlie was thriving and having the time of his life, they ended the conversation. Both were relieved that the warning had been delivered.

After hanging up the phone, Grandpa Wilson immediately made a call to the railroad station where Tommy was working that afternoon. With any luck he would probably catch him before the afternoon train arrived and Tommy would be out on the platform unloading the baggage. After only three rings, it was Tommy himself who picked up the receiver and answered.

"I'm so relieved that I got through to you, son, because I just had a call from Charlie's dad. There seems to be a problem and we need to get Charlie out of town for a few days."

It didn't take Wilbur long to explain to Tommy that the gang of men involved in the lynching could be looking for Charlie and seemed to have knowledge that he was possibly staying in Quinnimont.

"It's important that we get Charlie out of town immediately, so I want you and Dave to take him camping for a few days," he explained. "I'll arrange for you to have time off from your job, so when you finish unloading Number Thirteen's mail and baggage, come right on over here and I'll give you some money to buy everything you need for the time you'll be away."

"Where do you think we should go, Dad?" asked Tommy. "What would be the best place? Up on the mountain, perhaps?"

There was a pause as his father considered the possibilities. "Do you still have that boat you bought last fall?"

"Sure," Tommy answered. "Do you want us to take Charlie down river somewhere?"

"No. Actually I was thinking that perhaps the most isolated location would be right across the river on the Raleigh County side. No one lives over there and it's difficult to reach other than by boat. You would have the place all to yourselves and Charlie couldn't be safer anywhere else."

The decision had been made. "That's a great idea! I'll come on over as soon as I get through here," Tommy replied as he hung up the phone.

In less than an hour, Tommy was at his dad's house to pick up the money for the necessary supplies for the camping trip. He hadn't had a chance to talk to Dave yet about coming along, but his brother was on summer vacation so there would be no problem. Dave was always ready to just pick up and go on a minute's notice.

Mr. Wilson had a few final instructions for Tommy. He cautioned him to keep Charlie out of sight at all times and then added, "When it's safe for the three of you to come back across the river to Quinnimont, I'll tie a red flag on the big oak tree on the riverbank near where we had the baptism. I'll use one of the railroad signal flags that we have at the station. And don't forget to hide the boat. The three of you should be able to drag it up into the brush."

With the money from his dad in his pocket, Tommy headed on over to the company store. On the way there he spotted Dave at the ball field hitting some fly balls with a couple of his friends. Delighted that he didn't have to search all over town his brother, he called him over and quickly told him about the camping trip and the need for secrecy.

"This should be lots of fun," Dave said. "I've been wanting to spend some time over on that side of the river for a long time. Do you remember hearing about that woman who was captured by the Shawnee Indians and later escaped? People believe that she found her way back home to Virginia by following the river. Do you remember, Tommy?"

"Yeah, I think I do remember something about that. What was her name anyway?" Tommy asked.

"Mary Draper Ingles. And she probably traveled along the same side of the river where we'll be hiding out," Dave concluded. "Maybe we'll find some Indian relics. It's going to be great. Come on, let's go tell Charlie! He's going to be really excited. We can go to the store later."

As the two brothers started to walk away together, Dave stated, "Let's be sure to remember to take our swimming trunks. We'll have lots of time to go swimming. And we don't want to forget all the fishing gear. Yep, we're going to have a great time on this camping trip. And hey, be sure to take plenty of matches with us."

Tommy laughed. "Don't worry, little brother. We won't forget anything, not even Charlie! Let's be sure we don't forget Charlie!"

Hopefully they would all still be laughing after a few days of camping in the wilderness on the other side of the river.

CHAPTER 11

The Other Side of the River

Just as Dave predicted, I was really excited about the prospect of going camping with my two uncles. We spent the rest of the day gathering all the gear we would need for the camping expedition: tent, blankets, cooking utensils, lanterns and even an axe. The list seemed to go on and on. I guess it was better to take too much than too little.

By three o'clock when everything was piled up on the back porch, Grandma asked us this important question, "What are the three of you going to eat while you're away?"

"Gosh," said Tommy, "we hadn't even thought about that. Will you help us make a list? Dad gave me ten dollars earlier to buy what we need at the company store, but we got so involved in everything else that I completely forgot about getting the food."

With Grandma's help, a list of groceries was soon completed and the three of us trudged off to the store to purchase everything that was needed.

I could hardly sleep that night because I was so excited about going camping. I had never really been camping before. Sure, Bobby and I had slept out in the back yard at home a few times, but that didn't really count as camping. This was going to be the real thing.

Dave woke me really early the next morning before the sun even came up. Usually I hated to get up in the morning, but this was different. This was the day we were leaving for the other side of the river. Grandma was up early too and I could hear her in the kitchen fixing us breakfast.

There was still a lot to do before we could actually shove off. First we had to haul all of our supplies down to the river where Tommy's boat had been pulled up out of the water onto the shore. Even though we used Grandpa's wheelbarrow, we still had to make three trips to get all the gear down to the river. When everything was loaded, I actually wondered if there was going to be room in the boat for the three of us.

"Come on, Charlie," Tommy said. "Let's make a quick trip back up to the house and let Grandma know that we're on our way."

It was hugging and kissing time again and Grandma even prayed over us asking that the Lord would keep us safe and free from harm.

Just as we turned away and started back down to the river, Grandma suddenly asked, "How much water are you taking with you?"

Tommy and I just looked at each other in surprise.

"Water? We're not taking any water," Tommy replied.

"Well, if I were you, I'd certainly take some," Grandma advised us. "Until you find a spring where you can get some drinking water, you're going to need to have some water available. You'll get deadly sick if you drink the water from the river without boiling it first. It certainly won't hurt to take a couple of gallons along with you just in case you need it."

I took the big bucket and went down to the spring where we always got our drinking water while Tommy went to look for some containers in the shed. There was a pump in the house that supplied most of the water we used, but water used for cooking and drinking had to always come from the spring. Granddad was always talking about running a pipe from the spring to the house, but the work had never been done.

Grandpa also had elaborate plans for an indoor toilet. He had even built a small room off of the porch to house it, but a sewer line had to be dug first. That was to be Tommy and Dave's job, but although everyone talked about how great it would be to have an indoor commode, it just never seemed to happen. My mother always said that things moved slowly when you lived in a small town.

The sun was high in the sky by the time we finally had everything in the boat and were ready to shove off. Suddenly Dave suggested that I put on my swimming trunks.

"Why? We aren't going swimming, are we?" I asked.

"We're not planning to, but you never know when the boat might tip over. We've got a lot of stuff in there and it looks like the boat will be riding mighty low. Tom and I are going to wear our trunks," Dave replied.

"Well, okay, that sounds like a pretty good idea," I mumbled as I went into the bushes to change. While I pulled on my trunks, I began to pray that the boat wouldn't sink because I didn't know how to swim. I was actually even a little afraid of going out on the boat. Of course, I hadn't admitted that to my uncles. The last thing I wanted was for them to think of me as some kind of sissy.

A short time later we were all settled in the boat and ready to cast off. As we rowed away from the shore, Tommy was at the oars and Dave and I were sitting together in the back. I was just starting to relax when Dave suddenly shouted, "Look at that!" and pointed back to the shore.

As I looked around to see if something had been left behind, he grabbed my feet and flipped me backward out of the boat into the deep water. I panicked and began to fight the water as I felt myself going under. I starting kicking and beat the water with my hands, finally coming up to the surface screaming, "Help! Save me! Lord Jesus, save me!"

I could hear Tommy shouting at me. Over and over he was saying, "Come on, Charlie! Swim! You can do it! I know you can do it!"

"Glub, glub," I sputtered as I came up to the surface again spitting up a mouthful of water.

Clearly their words of encouragement echoed across the water. "Use your hands and kick your feet! Don't fight it! Come on, you're doing great, Charlie. Just keep on going."

I found myself relaxing under my uncles' coaching. Maybe I wasn't going to drown after all. The boat was only a few feet away from me and surely they weren't going to let me go down for the third time. I kept up the kicking with my feet and started moving my hands out in front of me. I was actually splashing along through the water following the boat.

After what seemed like a hundred years, the boat came to a stop. As I reached out to grab hold of the back of the boat, my feet touched bottom. I was safe! No one had to rescue me after all. I had actually been swimming.

Tommy had a big smile on his face. "Look back and see how far you swam today. That's quite an accomplishment for your first swim."

As I glanced back to where he was pointing, I saw the place we had shoved off from earlier. It was hundreds of yards across the river. Had I actually made it that far without drowning? It was like a miracle.

What an amazing experience. Of course, the boat had never been more than a yard or two ahead of me and Dave was always right there if I had really needed help, but I had done it! I don't think that I swam with any great form, but I had actually been swimming. When my two uncles had tossed me out of the boat, it was either sink or swim. They had it planned all along. I didn't know whether to be mad at them or to thank them for the swimming lesson. I decided to thank them.

"You also probably need to thank the Lord, Charlie," Tommy said. "I heard you praying out there and asking Him to save you. You learned two important lessons today. Number one, when you're in trouble, call on the name of the Lord. And number two, when you're in over your head, start swimming."

In the next couple of days, my uncles taught me a couple of strokes and how I should kick my feet to propel myself quickly through the water. I now was qualified to be called a swimmer. It was one of my great accomplishments of the summer.

Of course, I learned a lot of other things on the camping trip too. Tommy and Dave were not only fun companions, but also great teachers. My fishing skills improved, and after much practice I could start a fire just by rubbing two sticks together. I could identify poison ivy, put up the tent in record time, climb up and down the hilly pathways with ease and even fry a fish over the camp fire. These were things I could have never learned in Lee's Junction. Although we never found any evidence of the journey that Mary Draper Ingles had taken two hundred years before, I did find a really great Indian arrowhead along a trail one day. What a treasure!

It was fun to sit around the campfire at night under the stars and listen to Tommy and Dave weave their tall tales. They had almost as many stories to tell as Grandpa did. Oh, I almost forgot, Dave taught me how to play a harmonica and promised he would buy one for me when we got back to town. But I must admit that I really didn't care if we never got back to town. I was definitely having the time of my life with my uncles and I didn't want the camping trip to ever end.

One afternoon Dave caught a rabbit in a trap he had set and then skinned it so we could have it for dinner. I wasn't so sure how I felt about eating a rabbit because I used to have a pet rabbit that I kept in a pen back home. It had been given to me as an Easter present and I had really loved that rabbit. But Dave said I should just pretend that I was eating a piece of chicken and I must admit that it tasted pretty good.

My uncles never forgot for a minute that there was a possibility that my life might be in danger. They were always jumping up if they heard a strange noise or if they noticed another boat out on the river. Our boat had been pulled way up on shore and dragged into some bushes. Tommy wasn't taking any chances on it being spotted and had covered it with pine branches. We were camped pretty deep inland near the foot of a the mountain, but every day Dave or Tommy would go to the beach to see if Grandpa had put up the red flag as a signal that we should come back home.

I wasn't allowed to go out on the beach at all. We had found a spring not far from our campsite where we would get our water each day and a really great swimming place was located just a short walk from there. So whenever we would go to get fresh water, we would also trek on over to the secluded pool for a swim. That's actually where I learned to float and do the breast stroke. But Uncle Tommy said the pool was more than just our swimming hole. He said it was our bathtub too and was always passing me the bar of soap when we were there and reminding me not to forget to wash behind my ears.

As time passed, I was sort of hoping that the red flag would never be hoisted because I wanted our camping trip to last for a long time. But on the afternoon of the eighth day, Dave came running back to our campsite and said that the flag was up. It was safe for us to return to Quinnimont.

It had been a great adventure, but I guess that all good things have to come to an end. I felt kind of sad as we loaded up the boat for the return trip. Of course, it would be good to see Grandma and Grandpa again, but nothing could compare with my time on the other side of the river. I felt like I had grown up a lot being around my young uncles. They had treated me like I was one of the guys and not like some little kid.

And I had felt really safe on the camping trip. I had almost been able to forget the night of the lynching and what I had seen from the window. I wondered if the bad men were still looking for me or if perhaps the police had arrested them and they were all in jail.

As we climbed into the boat, I wondered how much longer I would be staying in Quinnimont. Perhaps everything was back to normal and I would soon be going home. For the first time in over two weeks, I felt a twinge of homesickness and wanted to see my parents again. I couldn't wait to tell Mom and Dad all about the camping trip and that I had learned how to swim. They would sure be excited about that news and Bobby would be really surprised too. Maybe we could even go swimming together when I got back to Lee's Junction.

Chapter 12

Stranger in Town

When we finally got back to Quinnimont and had all the gear stored away, Grandpa took us aside to fill us in on what had happened since our departure.

"It's a pretty long story, "he told us. "Sit down here and let me tell you about the visit that Alvin Billows paid to Quinnimont while you were away."

Grandpa told us that only two days after we had left on our camping trip, a man had shown up in Quinnimont riding a big red motorcycle. The stranger had pulled up in front of the company store, revved his bike and then shut down the engine. After looking around for a few minutes, he went inside the store and purchased a Moon Pie and a large orange soda and then attempted to strike up a conversation with the clerk who waited on him.

Apparently he asked some questions about the town, wanting to know the population and whether there were many visitors that came through Quinnimont.

The clerk had been warned by the railroad detectives not to respond to any questions about visitors, so he simply answered that no one ever visited Quinnimont and that even the locals were always talking about leaving the town. He said it with a smile like he was making a little joke.

The biker just sort of nodded and then asked where the post office was located. To his surprise the clerk simply turned and pointed to the far corner of the store where there was a row of combination-lock mailboxes next to a small barred window.

As the stranger started toward the window, the clerk called out, "Hold on a just a minute, sir. I'll be right on over there to open up for you."

Obviously the visitor wasn't used to small town ways where the store attendant was also the postmaster.

"I was just looking for some information," Alvin said. "There's no need to open up. A friend of mine wrote me a letter recently and it was postmarked from here in Quinnimont so I thought perhaps he might be staying here."

"Well, there's not really any place to stay in town. We haven't got a hotel. Maybe he was on one of the trains that stopped here. There's a mailbox down at the station and your friend could have dropped his letter in that box," the clerk suggested.

"Yeah, I guess that sounds reasonable. That's probably what happened. Thanks for your help."

Alvin gave a nod of his head, left the store and headed out to where he had left his bike. Just as he was about to pump the starter, he felt a hand on his shoulder. Turning, he saw a large man standing beside him with a badge pinned to his shirt and wearing a pistol on his hip.

"Sorry to bother you, but I wondered what your business was here in town. We don't have many strangers coming through," the officer said to the biker.

Alvin tried to remain calm. "Uh-uh, I just stopped in the store here to get me a Moon Pie and something to drink. I'm just passing through and I ain't done nothing wrong," he stammered. "Actually I'm just getting ready to leave town right now."

"What's your name and where are you from?" the official inquired

Alvin was really put on the spot. He certainly didn't want to tell anyone that he was from Lee's Junction, so he just decided to lie and replied, "I'm Alvin Billows from....Covington, Virginia."

"And what county is Covington located in?"

Alvin hesitated not having the vaguest idea of Covington's county. "Uh-uh, it's in Bath County."

The detective knew he was lying because Covington is actually in Allegheny County, but there was no reason to hold him. Although he suspected that Alvin was up to no good, he said, "Okay, best you be on your way now."

Climbing onto his bike, Alvin remarked, "Sure, I'm going. This ain't my kind of town anyway." He rode off with no intention to ever return.

The railroad detective noted that the license plate on the back of Alvin's motorcycle was from Virginia and at the bottom of the plate was clearly written the word "Stuart," denoting that it had been issued in Stuart County. Getting out his note pad, he wrote down the plate number and went immediately to call the Virginia State Police with his information on Alvin Billows.

"So that's pretty much the whole story," Grandpa told us. "A short time later the railway detective gave me a call and told me about his encounter with Alvin Billows. He assured me that he had already talked with the state police in Virginia and that everything was being checked out."

"So then I called your dad," Grandpa added, "and told him about Alvin's visit to town and about the questions that he had asked concerning your letter postmarked from here. One thing we know now is that we have to be much more cautious about letters and phone calls."

The good news was that Dad and Grandpa had decided that I was probably safer in Quinnimont than if I went back home to Lee's Junction. It was unlikely that Alvin would show his face again in town after his confrontation with the law and perhaps he had been satisfied with the answers that the clerk at the store had given him. So far, no one had been directly linked to the jailbreak and lynching. It was possible that things were quieting down. It was really just a time to wait and pray.

That night when I got into bed, I wasn't thinking about the bad men and the horrible things I had seen when I had looked out of the window. Instead my mind was filled with great memories of the camping trip and all the good things that were happening in my life. And best of all, I would be staying a while longer in West Virginia. This was turning out to be the best summer of my whole life.

CHAPTER 13

Show Time

The next day on my way to the company store to buy some groceries for Grandma, I noticed that someone had put up posters on almost every tree and electric pole in town advertising some sort of traveling show that would soon be coming to town. Each poster read:

SILAS GREEN
from
NEW ORLEANS
Minstrel Show
coming soon
to a local location

There were pictures of men and women in blackface dressed in fancy colored costumes. Hand printed in bright green letters at the bottom of each poster was the information that the show was going to be held on the ball field in the middle of town in just two days.

I quickly bought the things that Grandma needed and hurried home, only stopping to read the poster carefully once again. "What's a minstrel show?" I wondered. I had never heard of anything like that and was anxious to get back to Grandma's with the groceries to see if she could shed any light on the subject for me.

While Grandma put away the things I had purchased at the store, she told me all about the show that was going to be presented.

"These folks come to town just about every year at this time and they sing and dance and tell funny jokes. But I guess my favorite part is when they all get in a long line and ask silly questions of the fellow in the middle. They call him Mr. Interlocutor."

Grandma started smiling and I guessed she was remembering back to the last time the minstrel show was in Quinnimont. "The man in the middle is kind of the lead character and it's lots of fun for everyone to see and hear."

My grandma even was chuckling a little as she continued talking. "Folks come from miles around to gather under the big tent. Oh, Charlie, you would really enjoy this show. I'll ask your grandpa if he thinks it's all right for you to go."

I could hardly wait for Dave to come home so I could ask him all about this Silas Green Show that was coming to town. He had left early that morning to do some fishing on New River where he hoped to catch some smallmouth bass. I sat out on the porch in the rocking chair to await his arrival. Finally I spotted him coming up the street with a stringer of several fish and ran out to meet him.

"Dave," I shouted excitedly, "did you see the posters in town? Silas Green is coming here in just two days. Grandma's been telling me all about the show and she said that maybe I could go. Have you ever been to see it?"

"Sure, Charlie, I've seen it lots of times. I go every time the show comes to town even though they keep telling the same old jokes that I've heard so many times before. I really like their singing and dancing. I can guarantee that you'll have a great time there."

I noticed that there was a big smile spreading over Dave's face. It seemed like everyone who talked about Silas Green's show started smiling. In fact, I felt like smiling too and I hadn't even been to the show yet.

"Say, I have an idea," Dave said. "Maybe we can get you a job selling boxes of candy and Cracker Jack at the show. Would you like that? You might make a couple of dollars and I'm sure you can always use a buck or two extra in your pocket."

My ears perked up. "What do you mean? Someone would actually hire me to sell candy and Cracker Jack?"

"It's a possibility," Dave responded. "Every year the owners of the show choose several kids to walk through the crowd selling those things. You'd be surprised how many folks buy the Cracker Jack because of the prize that's in every box. Usually it's just a whistle or a tiny little doll or some junky thing. But every now and then someone actually finds a silver dollar or a watch in their box."

"And they actually pay kids to sell the stuff?" I asked.

"They sure do. You'll have fun and also make a little money on the side. And the best part is that you would get into the show for free."

Dave paused for a minute when he remembered that going to the show would expose me to a lot of people. "Of course, I'll have to check with Grandpa and see if he thinks it will be okay for you to go, but I don't believe it will be a problem. There will be hundreds of people at the show and no one's going to notice another kid there in the crowd. Sometimes the best place to hide is in the midst of a lot of people," he added.

"Anyway, as soon as the tent goes up, we'll go on down there and get you a job. The guy who does the hiring will remember me from last year because I recruited four boys to work for him," Dave told me. "He even gave me five dollars for helping him find the kids to sell the candy."

After talking with Dave, I started counting the hours until the show would come to town. Apparently posters had also been put up over in the neighboring town of Prince and even as far north as Layland. I hoped that Grandpa would give his permission for me to go. In fact, I even prayed and asked God to please move on my granddad's heart so that I could go see Silas Green from New Orleans and sell Cracker Jack and candy to the crowd.

We were eating breakfast two days later when Tommy came in after unloading the baggage from the morning train and told us that the show people had arrived in their green and gold trucks and were putting up their big tent.

"Hurry up and finish your breakfast," I urged Dave. "We need to get down there and see about the job. What if some other kids get there first?"

My uncle pushed his chair away from the table leaving his uneaten eggs and bacon still on the plate. "Okay, let's go. I'll race you to the ball field."

So we were off and running. As we approached the ball field the big green and gold striped tent was just about ready to be raised up on the three gigantic poles. Workmen were everywhere pulling on ropes and driving stakes. Everyone had a job and knew exactly what to do and when to do it. They all worked together like a well-oiled machine.

We didn't interrupt them in their work, but just stood by and watched. When a break was called so everyone could catch their breath, Dave spotted his friend from last year getting a drink of water.

"Hey, Butch! Remember me?" Dave shouted out.

You could tell that the fellow recognized my uncle immediately. "Sure, you recruited some kids to help me out last year. Yeah, I remember you. Those boys were all good workers too," he replied.

"Well, I have your first helper right here with me. He's a good worker and can shout really loud. He's probably going to be your best salesman this year."

Butch looked me over carefully. "Do you really think that you can sell candy, kid?"

"Yes, sir! I know that I can sell a lot of candy and Cracker Jack," I answered. "You can count on me."

"Okay then, you're in. The show starts at seven o'clock tonight so you need to be here by six-fifteen. Just ask for Butch. Everyone knows Butch. That's me," he stated positively. And giving me a pat on the shoulder, he turned away and headed off to where the tent was being erected.

I could hardly wait to get back to Grandma's house and tell her that I actually had a job for the next two nights with the Silas Green Show.

"A job, you say? Are they going to put you in blackface and have you out there singing and dancing?" Grandma joked.

"No, ma'am," I laughed. "I'm going to be selling candy and Cracker Jack and Dave says I will probably make two dollars a night."

I was so excited I could hardly contain myself. I had never had a real job before. My mother sometimes called taking out the garbage a job, but it wasn't a real job. With a real job you get paid and my folks didn't pay their own kids for doing what was expected of them around the house. But this was different. I was going to be working for the Silas Green from New Orleans Minstrel Show. It didn't get any better than that.

At promptly six-fifteen that evening I arrived at the big tent. My hair was all slicked down and I was wearing a clean shirt and my best pair of blue jeans. It didn't take me long to find Butch standing by one of the green trailers parked in back of the tent.

"Mr. Butch! I'm here to sell candy for you," I announced.

He once again looked me over very closely. For a minute I thought that he might even check behind my ears, but of course he didn't. Instead he reached into a box beside him and handed me a green apron with two large pockets on the front. He told me that one pocket was for folding money and the other for change.

"Both the candy and the Cracker Jack sell for twenty-five cents a box. The candy is salt water taffy and if anyone asks, you can tell them it comes directly from Atlantic City," Butch instructed me.

And then he told me exactly what I should do to sell my wares. I was to walk through the section I would be assigned and shout, "Candy! Cracker Jack! Get your candy and Cracker Jack here! There's a prize in every package!"

"Do you think that you can remember that?" Butch asked.

"You bet I can," I replied. "I'll be really loud."

And then I thought that perhaps I should demonstrate what a good salesman I could be, so I lifted up my voice and shouted at the top of my lungs, "Candy! Cracker Jack! Get your candy and Cracker Jack here! A prize in every package!"

I could tell that Butch was really impressed. "Well, okay! That sounds great. Everyone will certainly hear you. No doubt about that."

Leaning down and talking to me in almost a whisper, Butch continued with my instructions. "Now listen closely to what I'm about to tell you. This is really important. Here are two specially marked boxes of candy and Cracker Jack. Put them in the back of your case separate from all the others. You're to sell this one, this special box of candy here, to the guy with red hair who will be wearing a green plaid shirt. And the special Cracker

Jack box you are to sell to the lady with long blonde hair who will be wearing a bright blue dress."

I knew that what he was saying must be really important because Butch repeated it a second time. "Remember now, the man with the red hair and green plaid shirt gets the special box of candy, and the lady with the blond hair and blue dress gets the marked Cracker Jack box. Have you got that?"

"Yes, sir!" I replied.

"All right then. You get two cents for every box you sell tonight. Here's your merchandise case. It's not heavy and there are handles on both sides," he informed me. "As soon as the crowd begins to come in, you start selling the boxes. Remember, the guy will ask for the candy and the lady for the Cracker Jack. Don't give those special boxes to anyone else. Understand?"

"Yes, sir, I understand. I won't forget," I assured him as I tied on my money apron. I found four quarters for change in the one pocket and nothing in the other. Leaving Butch, I waited outside the main entrance for the crowd to start filtering in.

At six-thirty sharp the loudspeakers were turned on and the ticket seller began his chant, "Tickets! Get your tickets here!" The people began streaming onto the ball field and it seemed like everyone in town was coming. I wondered if there would be anyone left for tomorrow's show.

When the seats were about a third full, I began to sell my wares. To my surprise, almost everyone wanted a box of candy or some Cracker Jack. Half of my boxes were gone before the seats were even filled. I think that most folks were more interested in looking for their prize in the box than eating the candied popcorn or taffy. But I didn't really care if they ate it or not. What really mattered was that I was doing a great business.

Just about that time I heard a lady with very blonde hair and a bright blue dress calling out to me, "Boy! Come over here,

Boy! I want a box of Cracker Jack." She was waving her hand in the air to attract my attention.

As I made my way over to her, I was careful to be sure I picked out the special box to give her. The lady handed me a dollar bill and waited patiently while I made change for her.

As I walked away and started moving down the center aisle again, suddenly I heard her loudly exclaim, "Wow! Look at this! A brand new silver dollar. I found a silver dollar in the box!"

Everyone looked her way. You could almost feel the excitement rise in the crowd. My wares began to sell even faster than before. And it was only a few more minutes until a red-headed fellow wearing a green plaid shirt shouted at me, "Here, kid! I'll take a box of that salt water taffy."

As he flipped me a quarter, I passed him his box of candy and quickly moved on to serve another customer. And then it happened. There was a loud shout from the man with the red hair that immediately drew everyone's attention. He was actually standing on top of his seat and yelling, "Look at this! An Elgin wrist watch! It was in my box! I just got a real wrist watch!"

Talk about fast sales. People were lining up to buy my boxes of candy and Cracker Jack now. In fact, I had to hurry back to the trailer to reload before the show even began.

When the lights dimmed and the band began to play, I found an empty seat where I could sit down and watch the show. I hardly know how to describe it. The whole cast was wearing sparkly costumes from the gay nineties while they sang, danced and told corny jokes. Everyone in the audience laughed and clapped and sometimes even stood up and cheered. I guess when you work in the coal mines day after day, there isn't too much diversion and you need a time when you can just get away from it all.

When the show was finally over, I went back to the trailer to report in to Butch and give him all the money I had collected. Both pockets of my apron were nearly full and every box had been sold.

"Well, it looks like you did a great job tonight, kid. Do you want to come tomorrow night and help out again?" Butch asked.

"Yes, sir! That would be great. Do you want me at the same time?"

"Same time and same place. And here's the money that you earned tonight," he said, placing two one dollar bills in my hand.

Just as I was walking away, I noticed that the red-haired guy in the green plaid shirt had come over to Butch. I was still close enough that I could plainly hear what he was saying.

"Here's your watch back, Butch. I'll be in the same section tomorrow night and I'll be wearing a wearing a white shirt with a red tie. The boy you're using won't have any problem picking me out again."

I could hardly believe my ears. The whole watch and silver dollar thing had been a sham. It had all been faked so that people would buy more boxes of Cracker Jack and candy. And Butch had seemed like such a nice honest fellow to me, but then I guess that's show business.

The next evening at six-fifteen, I was back at the ball field to get my green money apron and the boxes of candy and Cracker Jack. People were already lined up at the main entrance waiting to purchase their tickets to the show. When they got to their seats, I was ready and waiting to start hawking my wares to all of my potential customers.

The whole evening was a repeat of the night before. The red-haired guy bought his special box of salt water taffy from me and I heard him shout out, "Wow! Look at this! There's a gold pocket watch in my box!"

Shortly afterwards, the blonde woman got my attention and once again loudly asked for a box of Cracker Jack. I expected her to announce that she had found another silver dollar, but even I was surprised because the prize mixed in with her Cracker Jack turned out to be a gold brooch.

It's amazing how those old well-worn hawker tricks seem to fool people time after time. Needless to say, once again my sales greatly increased as soon as these two "chosen" people had discovered their hidden treasures.

The content of the show was exactly the same as the previous night and once again the tent was filled with laughter and applause throughout the whole performance. The Silas Green Show was a rousing success in little Quinnimont and I had earned four whole dollars on my first real job.

I got up really early the next morning and went down to the ball field for one last look at the Silas Green traveling show, but to my great surprise, the tent and all the vehicles were already gone. The only thing left behind was a lot of trash, especially a lot of empty boxes that had once contained salt water taffy and Cracker Jack.

CHAPTER 14

A Snake and the River Rats

I had just arrived back at the house when Dave came out of his bedroom rubbing his eyes. "Where have you been so early in the morning?" he asked me.

"I've just been down to the ball field for one last look at the Silas Green Show, but would you believe that they have already packed up and left," I informed him.

"Yeah, they don't stay around long after the final performance. I suppose they have to get back on the road to set up for another show tonight. It's a pretty hard life, I guess," Dave concluded.

I was still thinking about everything that I had seen and done over the past two nights. "Silas Green from New Orleans." I repeated the phrase a few times to myself. It was almost like saying a little poem. How lucky can a guy be? I was here in Quinnimont at just the right time. If I had stayed home in Lee's Junction, I would have missed the whole thing.

I trudged on out to the outhouse, wondering when Grandpa was going to finish the plumbing for the indoor toilet. I hated everything about the outhouse, especially the wasp's nest that was up in the corner. The outhouse was the worst part of staying with my grandparents.

I heard Dave calling from the house. "Hurry up, Charlie. If you're going with me, we need to get moving."

He didn't need to call twice. "Just a minute. Don't leave without me." I was always ready to go anywhere with Dave. He was one of my very favorite people.

"Where are we going?" I asked.

"We have to go down and pick up the trash from the baseball field and then get it ready for our game this evening. There are always some pop bottles that have been left behind and we can redeem them at the store for two cents each," he explained. "If we're lucky, we might even find some money that people dropped on the ground during the last couple of nights. I guess you'd be interested in that."

"Sure I am. Who gets to keep the money we find?"

"We do. And also the money from the pop bottles," Dave informed me. "Get yourself some breakfast and we'll be on our way."

It didn't take me more than a minute or two to put some Corn Flakes into a bowl and pour a glass of milk While I was eating, Dave went out to the shed in back and found a couple of gunny sacks and two sticks with nails in the ends so we could spear the trash.

"Come on, Charlie," I heard him call. "We need to get to the field before anyone else if we're going to be first to find the empty bottles."

Quickly I left the house and rushed down the walk. Just as I started through the front gate, my foot came down on something soft and alive. Dave was right behind me and immediately realized what had happened and screamed, "Charlie, don't move! You've stepped on a snake."

I looked down and to my horror I saw that my bare foot was firmly planted right behind the head of a large, squirming snake. "Hold really still!" Dave cautioned. "Don't move a muscle! I'll take care of this. Just don't move!"

He took one of the sticks with a nail in the end that he was carrying and speared the snake right through its head.

"Now move real quick, Charlie! Jump back!" Dave instructed me.

And with that he jammed the stick with the nail and the wiggling snake impaled upon it right into the wooden gatepost. The snake's body struggled and squirmed, but its head was firmly nailed to the post and it couldn't get loose.

Shaking like a leaf, I asked, "What kind of snake is it?"

"Looks to me like a copperhead," Dave said. "You're really lucky."

As the two of us stood watching the snake's death struggle, a man from across the street called and asked, "What are you guys looking at there?"

"Some kind of snake that Charlie just stepped on and I jabbed with my stick," Dave replied. "I think it's a copperhead."

The man walked over, took a close look and confirmed the identification of the snake. "Boy, it's a good thing that you stepped on that there snake right behind the head. He couldn't bite you that way and Dave here was able to jam that nail right through its head. The good Lord must sure be watching over you today."

Meanwhile Grandma had heard all the commotion on the street and came running out. She almost fainted when we told her what had happened. She pulled me against her and hugged me so tightly that I could hardly breathe.

"You didn't even have shoes on today, Charlie," she observed.

"But Grandma, I've only worn shoes when I've gone to church. It's summer!" I replied.

Grandma was really upset about the snake incident. "I don't know how I would have explained to your parents if anything had happened to you," she muttered. "They sent you to us to keep you safe and free from harm and here you almost get bitten by a poisonous snake."

The neighbor said that snakes don't die until the sun goes down. I don't know if he really knew what he was talking about, but that snake sure did wiggle there on the gatepost for a long time.

Once the excitement was all over, Dave explained to me that the snake had probably just been sunning itself on the big flat rock just outside the gate. "It's really a miracle that you stepped exactly where you did," he surmised, "or else you would have been bitten for sure. This is really your lucky day."

Still talking about the snake, we headed off to the ball field and were happy to find that no one else had arrived there yet. There was lots of trash left behind by the patrons of the minstrel show and it was scattered all over the flat field. Watching the ground closely to be sure we didn't miss any lost coins, Dave and I stabbed every piece of paper and deposited it carefully in our bags. I almost found myself wishing that I hadn't sold so many boxes of candy and Cracker Jack because the empty boxes were everywhere.

And Dave had been right about it being my lucky day. I found three dimes, a nickel and two pennies while we were cleaning up. And it was an even luckier day for Dave who discovered a couple of dimes, a quarter and a shiny half dollar. But that wasn't all that we found on the ball field. We also picked up twenty-seven bottles that we could turn in to the company store for cash. Not bad for a couple of hours of work.

But then Dave informed me that the real work hadn't really begun. I wasn't sure what he meant until he brought out two long-handled rakes from a small shed at the side of the field. He also pulled out a really big flat piece of wood with short nails all along one side and a rope tied to both ends. I couldn't imagine what the purpose was for this unusual contraption, but I was soon to learn.

"This is what we use to drag the ball field," Dave explained. "We need to get it as smooth as possible for the game tonight. And then we have to pick up any rocks we find and toss them off the playing surface."

It was getting really hot by the time we finished raking and smoothing out the field and there was still a lot that remained to be done. We had to carefully line off the entire field with lime and hang red flags down each foul line. I decided that I definitely liked selling boxes of candy better than I did this hard manual labor, but I didn't want to complain and sound like a little whiny kid. And it was really fun working side by side with Dave.

My uncle Dave loved baseball. The whole time we were getting the ball field ready for the game, he was telling me all about their team, the Quinnimont River Rats, which I thought was a really cool name. Dave informed me that he was usually the starting pitcher for the team, but occasionally would play shortstop when he was needed in that position.

"Your Uncle Tommy, he's the catcher most of the time," Dave told me, "but every once in a while he's out playing in center field."

I laughed when Dave said that Tommy was called "Baldy" by all of his teammates. Tommy had shaved his head that summer, so I could certainly understand why he had been given that nickname. But then Dave explained that all of the members of the team had nicknames. When I heard what the other players were called, I laughed even harder.

Dave was known by everyone as "Hambone," which was often shortened to "Ham" or "Bone" by the other players.

Then there was "Stretch," another pitcher for the team who was really, really tall. Actually "Stretch" was six-foot-six and was the man who had been baptized in the river earlier that summer;

"Stilts" was at first base and had long skinny legs.

There was "Snuffy" in the outfield and "Wild Man" at third base.

"Boomer" was the outfielder and "Blinky" another catcher.

Two brothers, "Toad" and "Frog" played outfield and second base.

Finally there was "Boom-Boom," who was a utility infielder.

Dave told me all the real names of the eleven players, but I remembered them best by their nicknames. It was more colorful to think of the River Rats that way. The team had already won four games and lost only one, so they were having a really good season.

The game that evening was against the River Rats closest rivals, the Royals, from the neighboring town of Prince that was located just a mile west of Quinnimont. The team arrived in "royal fashion" with everyone riding in an old rusty pickup truck. Neither of the teams had official uniforms, but the players could easily be identified by the color of their baseball caps–red for the River Rats and purple for the Royals.

Both teams had a time of batting and fielding practice before the game began when the men shouted insults and snide comments back and forth. It was all done in good humor because the players, who ranged in age from about fifteen to thirty, were actually good friends who had known each other for a long time.

Since the two towns were so close together, the spectators at the game were about evenly divided when it came to cheering on their home teams. It was a friendly crowd where everyone seemed to know everyone else. All the folks had gone to the same schools, attended the same churches and many even worked at the same places, mainly for the railroad or the coal company. Quinnimont and Prince were about the same size and neither really had any industry to speak of. The elementary school was located in Prince and all of the kids from both towns attended there through the eighth grade. Everyone of high school age took a school bus up the mountain road to Mount Hope, a larger town located several miles away. It was a pretty tightly-knit community as you can imagine.

The folks in the two towns may have been good friends, but when it came to baseball, they were fierce rivals. You were for one team or the other. It was definitely the River Rats against the Royals.

Dave and Tommy pulled me aside shortly before the game started, informed me that I was to be the team's bat boy, and presented me with a brand new red baseball cap. It was my job to take care of the water bucket and bats, as well as to supply the umpire with spare baseballs when needed. Whenever one of our players got a hit or a base on balls, I was to run out, pick up his bat and bring it back to the bench.

As I put on my red hat, I felt like a real team player. What a great time I had that night. It was certainly a lot more fun to be a bat boy than a Cracker Jack salesman.

The game was really exciting with the River Rats prevailing by a score of ten to eight. The game only went for seven innings before the umpire called it because of darkness. The members of the teams then shook hands, patted each other on their backs and laughingly traded a few more insults. As the Royals drove off in their pickup truck, they could be heard shouting "We'll beat you next time!"

A few years later after high school, my Uncle Dave was offered a minor league contract by the Washington Senators. He played for several years with a few minor league teams, but never did make it into the majors.

CHAPTER 15

The Gunman

While all of this was happening in Quinnimont, the police investigation back in Lee's Junction was progressing without too much success. None of the actual perpetrators of the crime had been firmly identified. The police had a number of suspects, but none they could establish as definite members of the lynch mob. The families of the three Negroes who were lynched had moved out of town for fear that they too might meet with some untimely end.

The only name that the investigators really had was that of Alvin Billows, the fellow who had come to Quinnimont asking questions around town. Since I had positively identified him as one of the mob, the police were watching him very closely and making careful note of all his contacts.

Two of his known contacts were the postal clerk, Clarence Cogbill and a farmer by the name of Jasper Jenkins. However, since Mr. Jenkins seemed to have an unusually large number of visitors who stopped by his farm regularly, the police were keeping his place under almost constant surveillance.

The rumor had been spread around town that Jasper Jenkins was hosting poker games at his place. But instead of diverting suspicion, this had only caused the investigators to pay even closer attention to those visiting the Jenkins' farm because poker games in the county were illegal. The police began to refer to their growing list of Jasper's contacts as the Jenkins' group.

Because of my identification of Alvin Billows as a person definitely involved with the lynching, the police were keeping my dad aware of their findings. They strongly counseled my father that I should continue to stay with my grandparents in Quinnimont for a longer period of time.

The police further suggested that all communication with me by mail be very guarded. They were highly suspicious of Clarence Cogbill, the postal clerk, and believed that he was involved with those who were seeking to track me down.

A plan was devised where any letters to me would be addressed to my dad's father who lived in Hinton, West Virginia. Grandpa Bishop was an engineer on the C&O Railroad and regularly passed through Quinnimont on the trains he hauled. The idea was that he would receive any mail for me at his home address in Hinton and then drop it off with Grandpa Wilson on his next run. And he could also pick up any letters I might write back to my parents and post them at one of his other stops. It seemed to be the perfect solution. The police were being very cautious to keep my location secret.

Several of the Jenkins' group were also being watched very closely during the investigation. In fact, some of the gang began to suspect that the police had in some way linked them to the lynching and like all guilty people, they were constantly looking over their shoulders to see if they were being followed or were under surveillance.

Unknown to the authorities, the gang had decided that Alvin Billows should once again be dispatched to check out the

Quinnimont area since that was the only lead they had on where I might be staying. He was told in no uncertain terms to take care of that kid in the window and to make sure that I could never give testimony against anyone who was involved in the lynching. Since he had been the one careless enough to drop his hood that night, they felt he should also be the one to insure the removal of the witness.

In making preparations for his motorcycle journey, Alvin packed his .38-caliber snub-nosed pistol in his saddle bag along with some extra ammunition in case it was needed. If he found me, he was prepared to finish the job once and for all. He couldn't take any chances that I would ever appear on a witness stand.

It took Alvin nearly two days to reach Quinnimont. Along the way, he stopped for something to drink in a small coal mining town. The rundown cafe on the corner turned out to be a beer joint and the one beer Alvin meant to have quickly turned into six or seven beers. Staggering out of the dive an hour or two later, he felt a bit tipsy and ended up spending the night trying to sleep off the effects in a storm water culvert along the side of the road. As you can imagine, Alvin awoke early the next morning with a terrible hangover and it took him a couple of hours to find a place open where he could get a cup of coffee and an aspirin.

It was nearly ten o'clock when Alvin finally got to Quinnimont and he decided not to go down into town like he did on his previous visit, but choose to stay along Route 41 and conduct his surveillance from the hill, hiding behind the bushes that lined the highway. He had brought a cheap telescope with him from Lee's Junction and so he spent the rest of the morning observing every person who moved about town.

But I wasn't in town that morning. Tommy and I had left early and gone up Ewings Mountain, the mountain just across the creek from Granddad's house, to pick blackberries and we didn't return until mid-afternoon. The two of us actually got back just in time to get over to the ball field for that day's game. Alvin spotted us on the way to the field and immediately recognized me as the kid he had seen in the window on the night of the lynching.

There was no doubt in Alvin's mind that I was definitely the witness who had seen his face and could identify him. His orders were very clear. He was to shut me up for good. It was easy to say, but very difficult to accomplish. How could it be done? That was the question that Alvin pondered as the day wore on.

During the game, he was bold enough to come to the field and mingle in with the crowd that had gathered. Alvin observed my every move during the game and spied on me as I walked home with Dave and Tommy. It didn't take him long to determine the house where I was staying, but his problem then was how to get close enough to me to accomplish the job he had been sent to Quinnimont to do.

As the game was ending, Alvin quickly left the main part of town and headed back to his hiding place in the bushes. It was time to put his plan into action. He had decided to use his gun and finish me off under the cover of darkness. One shot should be sufficient if he could just get close enough to get his sights on me. Alvin's mind was made up and nothing was going to stop him. He had his mandate. He had been ordered to shut me up once and for all and that's what he was going to do. There was no way that he was going to allow me to ever take the stand to give testimony against him. It was either going to be him or me.

No one in the Wilson household was taking any special precautions that evening because we were completely unaware that any real danger was close at hand. Dinner was running behind schedule because Grandpa had worked late and my uncles and I had been at the game.

As darkness fell, Alvin apparently felt secure enough to venture down the hill into town and approach our house. His plan was to come down the alley in back of the house on foot, leaving his motorcycle hidden in the bushes up the hill by the highway. As he neared the house, we were all sitting at the dinner table and had just finished saying the blessing over the food.

As Alvin peeked in through the window, he immediately recognized me there with the others at the table. I had one elbow resting on the tabletop as I ate a butter-smeared ear of corn on the cob. Alvin decided not to wait for another moment but to shoot me there and then and have it over with. He pulled out his gun and took careful aim through the window. But just as he squeezed the trigger, I leaned forward to get another biscuit and his shot missed me completely.

When Alvin fired his pistol, the window shattered and the broken glass went flying everywhere. The noise sounded more to me like a stick of dynamite going off than a gunshot, but Grandpa knew a gunshot when he heard one. He shouted for everyone to get down, immediately turned off the lights and ran for his gun to go after the assailant. Tommy and Dave crawled across the room to the door, grabbing a flashlight along the way. However, Alvin had fled the scene as soon as his gun went off and hadn't even looked around to see if he had hit his target–ME!

My grandfather and uncles charged out the back door to search for the gunman and spotted him briefly in the alley just before he ran around the corner. Tommy and Dave ran ahead of Grandpa as he limped along behind and caught sight of the shooter briefly as he ran across the spur line. Alvin was last seen as he ducked under a coal car on the siding at the foot of the hill. When the trio of pursuers arrived at the spot where he had disappeared from view, they heard his motorcycle start up as he began to make his escape from the area.

Meanwhile, back at the house, Grandma quickly went over to the train station to inform the railroad police of what had happened. They, in turn, called the state police and the sheriff's office before driving my grandmother back home where together they awaited the arrival of the state police. It wasn't long before Grandpa returned with Dave and Tommy, but it was nearly an hour before the police finally came onto the scene.

Everyone was very concerned for my welfare and stated how fortunate it was that I happened to reach for another biscuit just at the right time. The police checked around the outside of the window for fingerprints and then found and extracted the slug of the bullet from the wall. They didn't have a camera, but instead made a drawing of the room, including where we were seated and where the gunman had stood outside of the window.

A footprint in some sand by the back gate was found by one of the police, but it was too vague to be of any great value as a clue. However, they did estimate that the footprint was made by a size twelve shoe, a shoe much larger than any worn by someone in our family.

One of the railroad cops suddenly remembered the suspicious fellow who had been in town a week or two previously and was able to provide the police with the motorcycle license plate number that he had carefully recorded in his note pad. The authorities both to the east and west along Route 41, which was the only road that passed through town, were quickly notified of this important piece of information.

That night no one in the house slept very soundly. Tommy and Dave took turns sitting in the living room on guard with Grandpa's gun on their laps and a flashlight close at hand.

I must admit that I have never been more afraid in my entire life than I was that night lying in my bed trying to fall sleep. The time when the mob was across the street at the jail house had been pretty scary, but at least they weren't shooting at me. What had happened at the dinner table earlier had left me terrified. I could have been killed. I felt cold and shaky, and even though it was warm in the room, I wrapped up in the cover. I guess I was looking for some kind of protection. What if the shooter came back and tried to shoot me again?

It must have been about three o'clock in the morning when Grandpa came into the room to check on me and saw that I still wasn't asleep. He prayed a short prayer asking the Lord Jesus to keep watch over me and keep me safe. Afterwards I felt much better and actually got some sleep for a couple of hours, but it was a very, very long night.

The next morning the police once again came to the house, this time bringing a whole list of questions that they wanted answered. Grandpa explained how I had witnessed the lynch mob taking the colored men from the jail back in Virginia earlier that summer and also informed them that apparently I was the only person who could positively identify even one of the abductors.

"We thought that Charlie would be out of harm's way staying here with us in Quinnimont," Grandpa said sadly, "but obviously we were wrong. It looks like someone has tracked him right here to this house."

The police seemed confident that the gunman would be caught, stating that an "all points bulletin" (or an APB as they called it) had been issued for Alvin Billows and his red motorcycle. They suspected that he would try to get back to Virginia by the shortest route possible, so policemen all along the main route would be keeping a sharp eye out for him.

One other thing they mentioned was that they had located a place where someone, probably the Billows fellow, had been watching the town from the bushes along the highway. They had come across some candy wrappers and a couple of empty beer bottles there which they had gathered up and were currently processing for fingerprints.

After the police finally left, Grandpa called Tommy, Dave and me into the kitchen for a serious talk about the situation. He felt that it might be best if the three of us got out of town immediately and thought that the answer might be for us to take another camping trip.

"How about if we go up onto Ewings Mountain and camp somewhere near the old hermit's place?" Dave asked. "No one would ever think to look for us up there."

It sounded pretty exciting to me. "What old hermit?" I asked. "I never heard anything about a hermit living up on that mountain."

"Oh, Dave's just talking about J.A.P. Ewings," Grandpa told me. "Folks around here call him "Jap" because of his initials. He's an old man that has a little hut on the mountain near a deserted coal mine. He's been living up there alone for years and claims that the mountain and all the coal under it belong to him. Jap's about as harmless as they come."

Grandpa paused as he considered Dave's idea. "I can't think of a safer place for you all to camp for a few days. I doubt if you'll even run into him while you're on the mountain, plus there's a good spring with fresh water."

So it was settled. Another camping trip was in order. Grandpa told us to get our gear together and then to make a quick stop at the store to get the food we would need. "Just tell the storekeeper to put it on my account."

But before we even had time to begin our preparations, the phone rang. It was the police informing us that they were on the trail of Alvin Billows. He had been spotted on US Route 60 going east toward the Virginia border. The Virginia State Police were going to set up a road block at the state line and the West

Virginia troopers were closing in on him from the west. Alvin would soon be in police custody and locked up in jail.

To say we were relieved at the news is probably the understatement of the year. The bad guy would soon be captured and we could all breathe easy again. But sometimes things don't work out the way you think that they will.

After hanging up the phone, Grandpa still thought that it was best that we continue with our preparations for the camping trip, however before we could even get out our backpacks, the phone rang again.

Once more it was the police with additional news about the manhunt. The troopers had apparently spotted Alvin Billows and began a chase with their patrol car. Somewhere on US 60 east of Sam Black's Church, the small town where my family had stopped for barbecue on the way to Quinnimont, Alvin had spotted the police on his trail. Turning his throttle up as far as it would go, he speeded up considerably in an attempt to stay ahead of his pursuers. But on the way down Muddy Creek Mountain, Alvin missed a steep turn and actually went airborne off of the road and into a thick rhododendron patch. His body flew off in one direction and his motorcycle in another. Alvin had landed perhaps a hundred yards away from the highway.

The police officers were attempting to get to him, but they were having a hard time cutting through the dense thicket. Everything had happened so quickly and the officers didn't really have the proper equipment to reach Alvin. In fact, no one was sure whether he was dead or alive.

Dave, Tommy and I stood by Grandpa as he listened to all the details over the phone. Of course, we could only hear one side of the telephone conversation and were struggling to make sense out of Grandpa's comments.

"Really? You don't say. Where did it happen? He landed where? Of course. Yes, he'll be here at the house. No problem."

Finally, Grandpa hung up the receiver and filled us in on the details of the chase and the accident as they had been related to him. We could hardly believe our ears. What an amazing turn of events.

"Charlie," Grandpa said to me, "the police want you to come to the scene of the accident and make a positive identification of the suspect. They need you to confirm that this is the same man that you saw outside of the jail, so they're sending over a police car to pick you up. It should be here in just a few minutes," he continued. "I'm going to send Tommy along with you. This should actually be pretty exciting as you'll get to ride in a police car and see all the gadgets. And they'll probably even be using the siren."

"Just a second, Grandpa," I replied with enthusiasm. "I need to go get my red baseball cap! I want to be ready to go when they come!"

Wow! I was really going to ride in a police car with the siren blaring. Another adventure was being added to my already excitement-filled summer.

CHAPTER 16

Positive Identification

It was a long half hour as I waited patiently for the state trooper to show up in his patrol car. Well, maybe I didn't actually wait so patiently since I was continually running back and forth to the window, listening for the sound of the siren that would announce the arrival of the police car.

Finally the policeman arrived and Tommy and I were ushered into the trooper's car and were on our way. The scene of the accident was over fifty miles away and it took us well over an hour to reach it. The mountain roads on Route 41 and US 60 were very steep with one hairpin turn after another. A couple of times I had to hold my breath because I thought we might actually run off the side of the road.

Apparently that's what had happened to Alvin Billows. Traveling down the mountain at a very high rate of speed in his attempt to outrun the police, he had made the first several turns, but missed the most dangerous one. His motorcycle had literally flown off the road and then went airborne down the side of the mountain landing in the dense undergrowth.

There were already three or four West Virginia State police cars on the scene when we arrived. I also counted two cars from the sheriff's office and three other emergency vehicles along the roadside. A group of men were busy attempting to make their way through the heavy brush to find Alvin. They had already come upon his motorcycle, but couldn't seem to locate him. Cutting a path through the dense vegetation was proving to be a very difficult job. The rhododendron intertwined in such a way that it formed an almost impregnable wall.

When they eventually found Alvin, he was in horrible shape. His clothing, even his leather jacket, was torn to bits and he had cuts all over his body. His head was lying at a terrible angle and at first glance there seemed to be no sign of life at all. But then the rescuers heard a faint moan coming from the injured man and a call went out to the nearest clinic in Rupert for a doctor to come to the scene of the accident immediately.

Those of us waiting at the side of the road for the doctor's arrival had no idea of what was really happening down there in the thicket. Every now and then someone would come out of the underbrush bringing us an update on Alvin's condition. All we knew was that he was still breathing and was in great pain.

A few people clapped when the doctor finally drove up. After talking briefly with the state troopers, the doctor crawled down the mountainside along the path cut through the thicket, dragging his black bag along with him. When he finally reached Alvin, it apparently took him only a minute to diagnose the main problem–a broken neck and probable brain damage. Apparently Alvin had been in such a hurry to get away that he hadn't been wearing his airplane cap with the goggles. His head was completely unprotected and had taken the brunt of the impact.

The doctor put out a call for a stretcher and a backboard and immediately began to minister first aid to the unconscious man. He didn't want Alvin moved until he could be stabilized. It was a slow and tedious job, but finally they had him ready to carry up to the highway and into the waiting ambulance.

Just as they were about to place Alvin into the vehicle, the officer who had driven Tommy and me to the accident scene led me over to the ambulance.

"Is this the man you saw the night of the lynching?" he asked.

Alvin was a mess, but through the bandages I saw the same man I had seen many times back home in Lee's Junction on his motorcycle. And there was no doubt in my mind that it was the same exact man that I had seen outside of the jail carrying a gun on the horrible night of the lynching.

Without hesitation I replied, "Yes, sir. I am sure that is Alvin Billows from Lee's Junction, Virginia. He is definitely the man I saw on the street outside of the jail that night."

Upon hearing my words, the policeman announced, "I am placing this man here under arrest for speeding and attempted murder. He is also to be held for the Virginia authorities who will be handling that case. The closest hospital is in Ronceverte, so let's get him over there as quickly as possible."

Tommy and I watched the ambulance start down the mountain road and then were quickly hustled into the police car that would follow as an escort for the emergency vehicle. I was starting to get a little tired of hearing sirens. The excitement had worn off and I was ready to get back to Grandma's house. It had been a long day already and it was only a little after noon.

By the time we got to the hospital and waited while the police made all the arrangements for Alvin to be admitted, another two hours had passed. We just sat on a hard bench outside of the emergency room entrance until I began to think that Tommy and I had been forgotten. But finally two policemen showed up and took us to a little cafe near the hospital where we had a sandwich and some ice cream.

While we were eating, they outlined their plans to get us back to Quinnimont. "We've decided that the best way for you to return home is on the evening train," the younger policeman explained. "Don't worry about anything. Arrangements have been made for you to stay at the hospital in the waiting room until it's time to take you to the station. A police car will pick you up in plenty of time to catch the train."

So after lunch it was back to the hospital and more waiting. Tommy actually dozed off and then there wasn't anything for me to do but just watch the big clock on the wall tick off the minutes.

I don't know how long it was until a nice looking gentleman with a stethoscope around his neck came into the room and walked over to us.

"Are you the two young men that came in with the man who was in the motorcycle accident?" he asked politely.

Tommy replied, "Yes, sir. I guess you could say that."

"My name is Dr. William LeHue and I'm the attending physician for the accident victim. Are you relatives?"

"No, we've never even met the man," Tommy informed the doctor. "But my nephew here knows a lot more about him than I do,"

Turning to me, the physician inquired, "What information can you give me, young man? Do you know his full name and how I can reach his family?"

"Well, it's a long story," I replied, "but I can identify him as a member of a lynch gang. And guess what? He tried to kill me last night."

"He did what? You're telling me that he actually tried to kill you?" The doctor seemed almost shocked speechless by what I had just told him.

"Yes, sir," I answered. "He fired a shot through the dining room window while I was eating, but he missed. I think the Lord must have been protecting me."

"You've got to be kidding? I can't imagine anyone actually trying to kill a little kid. How old are you anyway? About nine?" he asked.

"I'm actually only eight, but I'll be nine in September. And sure enough, that man in there really did try to kill me. It was pretty scary."

The doctor got really quiet. I think he was having trouble believing that his patient actually wanted to take my life. He finally nodded his head and I thought he was going to leave, but instead he continued on with our conversation.

"You never told me if you know the man's name and where he lives. The police weren't able to give us hardly any information about him except details on where the accident took place."

"I can tell you that his name is Alvin Billows and that he's from over in Lee's Junction, Virginia. That's where I live too, in Lee's Junction."

The doctor had taken a pad from his coat pocket and was writing down the information I was giving. He continued with his questions. "How about his family? Do you know how I can reach them?"

"I don't really know his family, but I do know that he has three brothers named Abner, Archie and Alex. They all live in Lee's Junction and they all ride motorcycles. I see them around town, but I can't say I really know them." I was trying to give the doctor as much information as I could

"Do you know if his family has a phone so that I can call them and let them know what has happened?" he asked.

"I really can't say for sure, but I expect they do. Most everybody in town has a telephone. You could contact the telephone operator. She knows everyone in Lee's Junction and what their numbers are."

I was trying to be as helpful as I possibly could be. "What I do when I need to talk to someone is to just give the operator their name and ask her to ring them. It's not really a problem."

Tommy finally broke into the conversation and explained to the doctor exactly what we were doing there in Ronceverte. He told him that the police had brought me to give positive identification that Alvin Billows was the man I had seen at the jail the night of the lynching.

"Very interesting," the physician replied. "I guess that explains why they have posted a police guard outside of his door. I'm definitely going to try calling the telephone operator in Lee's Junction as you suggested."

He started to leave and then turned back to me and said, "You say this man was part of a lynch mob? I'm sure that I read about that incident in the newspaper not long ago."

And with those words, he walked back down the hall, leaving us alone in the waiting room wandering how much longer it was going to be until we would be heading back home.

Over an hour passed before the state policeman who had driven us from Quinnimont to the accident scene arrived and asked, "Are you all ready to catch that train back home?"

Were we ready? We had been ready and raring to go for hours!

"Yes, sir," answered Tommy politely. "We are definitely ready."

The policeman drove us over to the train station. I was given a ticket, but Tommy, as an employee of the C&O, was able to use his rail pass.

When the train arrived, we took seats in the coach. I loved trains. Maybe it was because I was from a railroading family and trains were in my blood. At least that's what my mother always told me. In just a minute or two the train moved out of the station heading westward. I had just settled back in my seat when the conductor came through collecting tickets. I gave him mine and of course Tommy just presented his railway pass. The conductor examined his pass and asked, "Are you Wilbur Wilson's son, the former railroader who works at the station in Quinnimont?"

"Yes, sir, I sure am," Tommy replied. "And this here is his grandson, Charlie Bishop."

The conductor looked me over carefully. "Your last name is Bishop?" he asked. "Are you by any chance kin to George Bishop, the engineer?"

I stood to my feet and said proudly, "Yes, sir, that's exactly who I am. Actually, he's my other granddaddy!"

"Well, how about that," he responded. "Your grandpa is one of the best engineers I know and I have a surprise for you. He's the engineer driving this train you're on tonight. Isn't that a coincidence?"

With a big smile on his face, the conductor reached out to shake my hand. "I'll let him know that you're back here. He'll be taking us as far as Hinton tonight where we switch engineers. Glad to have you both aboard."

Mumbling something about collecting his tickets, he turned away and was off down the aisle.

We stopped in Hinton and I looked out the window to try to spot Grandpa Bishop, but it was dark so I never saw him. Then the train started up again and we continued on our way home. Actually it wasn't really my home because I was just visiting there, but in lots of ways it felt like home.

It was about midnight when we pulled into the station at Quinnimont and Tommy had to wake me up to get me off the train. I had been sleeping almost the whole time after we left Hinton. It had been a long, hard day. Grandpa Wilson and Dave were there at the station to meet us and listen to our adventures as we walked homeward. It was sure turning into an interesting summer vacation. I found myself wondering what was going to happen tomorrow.

CHAPTER 17

On Ewings Mountain

I woke up the next morning wondering if the camping trip that Dave and I had planned on Ewings Mountain was still going to take place. We had actually gathered all of our supplies before the police came to get me to identify Alvin Billows, but things had changed now and I was no longer in danger. With the gunman in the hospital under arrest, I knew that I would probably be heading home pretty soon.

But Grandpa had some good news when I got to the breakfast table.

"Dave and I were talking this morning and we know how much you're looking forward to that camping trip. What do you say that I call your dad and ask him if you can stay here a few more days? There's been so much excitement around here lately that a little time away on the mountain will be good for you."

When Grandpa came home from work that afternoon, there was a big smile on his face and I knew just from looking at him that my folks had agreed to let me stay. The camping trip was still on and we would be leaving in the morning. Dave told me that we would have to travel a lot lighter than when we crossed over New River to camp earlier in the summer.

"We're going to have to carry everything on our backs up the mountain and it's a pretty tough climb," Dave explained. "We don't want to take any more than we absolutely need for the three days we'll be away. I hope you're feeling strong because you're going to be toting a heavy pack."

We left shortly after daybreak and took the old logging road up the mountain. Dave said taking the road was a little longer, but it was an easier climb than some of the other routes which were much steeper. I was really glad that we weren't carrying a heavier load because I was exhausted when we finally reached the top of the mountain around noon. After a brief stop to eat the peanut butter and jelly sandwiches we had packed for lunch, Dave led us to a nice clearing, the perfect place to put up a lean-to. We weren't planning to build anything complicated and just collected some branches and limbs to use on our make-shift shelter.

When our sleep area was completed, we gathered rocks to make a fire pit. The last thing we needed was to have our cooking fire get out of hand and set the woods aflame. It was fun to cook our dinner under the stars. Grandma had given us a slice of ham which we warmed on a stick over the hot fire, and we opened a can of pork and beans to round off our meal. I was starting to feel like a real mountain man and an experienced camper.

Dave was teaching me all sorts of things. After we had finished eating, Dave told me to select a spot several yards away from our campsite and dig a hole to bury our garbage.

"We certainly don't want to attract any wild animals by leaving scraps above ground," he cautioned me. "I've heard that black bears have been seen in this area and we sure don't want any bears nosing around our camp."

Upon hearing about bears, you can be sure that I dug a really deep hole for the trash. After my experience with the snake in town, the last thing I wanted to encounter on the mountain was a bear. I wasn't taking any chances and pushing my luck too far.

Later that night we sat quietly by the fire and listened to the sounds coming from the woods and looked up at the display of stars covering the sky above us. Dave showed me how to locate the North Star by finding the Big Dipper and informed me that the Indians referred to the Big and Little Dipper as the Big and Little Bears. He also pointed out Orion, the Hunter, and several other constellations.

As we listened to the night noises that surrounded us on every side, Dave identified the sound of the owl and nightingale, as well as the crickets and frogs. It was like we were tuned into a symphony of sound.

"How do you know so much about all the stars and stuff like that?" I asked Dave, fascinated by the amount of knowledge he had.

"Your grandpa taught us boys about all sort of things. I remember that once he told us that the stars are kind of like God's angels watching over us and the constellations are special groups of angels. He has a special knack for making learning fun," Dave added with a smile.

It was fun to sit under the stars and talk to Dave sort of man to man. "Yeah, Grandpa is a really neat guy. I particularly like it when he tells me stories about the 'old days' when he played baseball. Did he actually ever play baseball?"

Dave sort of chuckled as he replied because sometimes Grandpa's stories were pretty far fetched. "He sure did. Your grandpa's the one who taught me how to throw a curve, a slider and a knuckleball. I'm better with the slider and curve than with the knuckleball, but Dad says that if I work at it maybe I can even make it to the big leagues someday."

"How about Grandpa? Did he ever make it to the big leagues?" I questioned.

"No, he never did," Dave continued. "The war came along and he always said that when duty called, he answered. And of course, then our family started to grow and he needed to work to provide for all of us."

Dave reached out and stirred the fire before adding, "But he taught all seven of us boys to play the game as we were growing up. And he was obviously a great coach because all of us are strong players on the diamond. In fact, I'm going to try for the big leagues in another year or so."

"I sure hope you make it," I told him. "It will be neat to tell all the guys that my Uncle Dave is a professional baseball player."

"Well, I hope you get the chance, but it's going to take a lot of work on my part and some really good luck to boot," Dave responded.

"Did you ever pray and ask the Lord to help you?" I suggested.

"No, can't say that I ever have, but maybe I should add some prayer into the mix," Dave said as he rose to his feet. "Come on, little nephew, let's see if there's enough room for both of us to fit into that lean-to."

It was pretty crowded when we bedded down for the night, but I felt mighty safe with Dave right there close beside me to protect me from any wild animals that might decide to visit our camp while we were asleep.

When I woke up the next morning, Dave already had the fire going and was getting things ready for breakfast. We held slices of bread over the fire to make toast to go along with the scrambled eggs he had made. Maybe the eggs weren't really that great, but I was so hungry that anything would have tasted good.

After we had cleaned up from breakfast, Dave suggested that we walk over to Jap Ewings' place so that I could meet the old miner. I had never met a real hermit and I was anxious to see if he looked any different than anybody else. I wasn't quite sure what to expect.

Jap's place was only about a half a mile from our campsite, a ten minute walk at a steady clip. As we stepped out of the woods into a clearing, Dave said, "That didn't take long. This is where Jap lives."

I looked around and I didn't see a house or anything. But then on closer observation, I saw a path at the edge of the clearing leading to what resembled a pile of logs. But it turned out that it wasn't a pile of logs at all. It was actually some sort of cabin. The structure blended so well with the woods that I might have walked right by and never even realized that it was someone's home.

Dave raised his voice and shouted, "Jap! Are you around here somewhere?"

Coming out from behind the log cabin, I heard a voice, "Yep, I'm here. Who's out there calling me?"

"It's Dave Wilson and I've got my nephew with me. Will you come on out so that Charlie can meet you?" Dave responded.

"Just a jiffy," the reply came. "I've been back in the mine hewing out some coal. Let me brush off some of the dust."

It wasn't long before an old man emerged dressed pretty much in rags. On his head he wore an old miner's cap with a carbide lamp attached to the front of it. Taking off his cap as he approached us, he put out the lamp. And as he did, I noticed that carved into the hard bill of his cap were the letters J-A-P.

The old hermit seemed friendly enough. "Good to see you, Dave. And you say that this here is your nephew, Charlie?"

"Yes sir. He's been visiting us from Virginia this summer," Dave answered putting his arm around me and pushing me forward a little.

"I been to Virginia once a good spell back," the man called Jap replied. "Went with my pappy. But I never been back and can't say that I recall much about the place."

"You look like you've been back in the mine," Dave observed.

"Sure 'nuf. Every once in a while I gotta dig me some coal for my stove and stock up for the wintertime. Gets pretty cold up here in the winter, you know," the hermit reminded us.

"So your mine is still producing?" Dave asked, more to make conversation than anything else.

"Yep, still a lot of coal in this old mountain. Every once in a while some fellow from this or that coal company comes by trying to get me to sign a paper that would allow them to dig on my mountain. But I ain't about to sign nuttin' allowing anyone to dig on my mountain," he declared. "Someone gotta keep nature as nature."

"That's certainly right, sir," Dave affirmed politely.

"You fellers just up here for the day, are ya?" Jap asked.

"Actually for about three days," Dave replied. "We're camped about a half a mile north of here in that big clearing near the spring. You know the place I mean? The same place I camped when I was up here last year."

"Sure," the old man responded. "You gave me some salt and sugar when you were leaving. I really appreciated that."

"Well, I hope you don't mind us using some of your land," Dave added. "It's really beautiful up here on the mountain."

"You're welcome up here anytime. You never cause a feller any problems. Enjoy my mountain while you're here. Just be sure you leave it like you found it when you take off," old Jap stated.

"We'll probably be breaking camp tomorrow about noon. We'll stop by on our way down to town. See you then," Dave said in parting. We looked back as we came to the edge of the clearing and waved at the old man. He lifted his hand and waved back.

"Right nice old fellow," I commented.

"Yeah, I think so too, but there are some folks around here who think he's crazy. He may be eccentric, but he's sure not crazy. That old man has more natural sense than most folks give him credit for," Dave informed me as we started back down the path to our campsite.

Then changing the subject and lowering his voice, Dave continued, "Let's try to be very quiet on the way back. If we don't make any noise, we just might see a deer or a fox or some other critter. There's a lot of wildlife here on the mountain and I'm surprised that we haven't seen any yet."

Attempting not to make a sound, we had walked only another fifty feet or so when Dave suddenly held up his hand and pointed over to the right. I looked in the direction he was indicating and there was a doe and her fawn feasting on a patch of grass. As we watched, a large buck with a beautiful rack of horns joined them. It was a sight to behold.

And then just a little further along the path, Dave stopped and pointed to the ground directly in front of us. At first I didn't see anything, but then suddenly I saw it right in the center of the path. There was a large paw print that was bigger than my hand. Looking closer, I saw that there was another print and then another. Something had definitely crossed our path.

"What kind of track is that, Dave?" I asked.

"It's the paw print of a bear. He's probably been out looking for his lunch. We'll just keep on going because he might like some fresh 'boy-meat' today. You don't want to become his meal, do you?" Dave replied laughing.

"No way! Let's just keep moving," I answered, speeding up.

That night for dinner we roasted hot dogs on sticks over the fire and warmed up another can of pork and beans. And for dessert? You guessed it. We roasted marshmallows on the hot dog sticks and drank tea from tin cups.

Once again I slept like a baby on my mattress of pine boughs, cuddled up next to Dave. Being in the lean-to was like being in a little nest and I felt safe and secure there with my uncle by my side.

We spent the morning close to the campsite and packed up after lunch. As promised, we cleaned up the area real good and buried all our trash in the garbage pit that I had dug. Finally we tore down the lean-to and headed over to Jap's place to tell him goodbye before starting down the mountain.

When we reached his clearing, we called out to Jap to let him know we were there, but there was no response. Dave suggested that we move closer and then he called out again, but there was still no response.

"Maybe he's back in the mine and can't hear us," Dave suggested.

As we approached Jap's cabin, Dave opened the door and shouted very loudly, "Jap! Jap! Are you in there?"

Very faintly we heard a reply, "I'm here, back in the mine. Help me! Please help me!"

I looked into the small room, but I certainly didn't see any mine or mine entrance. "Where's the mine?" I asked Dave.

"It opens right behind that blanket hanging there on the wall," he informed me. And sure enough, as Dave pulled the blanket aside, I saw the opening to the mine shaft right there inside of Jap's cabin.

"Where is he, Dave?" I inquired anxiously.

"He must be back in the mine somewhere," was his answer. "Do you see a lamp or something anywhere in the cabin? I must have some light."

I remembered that I had a flashlight in my pack that I had left just outside the door. "Can you use my flashlight?" I asked.

"Anything! Just get it quickly and bring it here," he ordered.

I ran as fast as I could, praying that it wasn't hidden under everything that I had crammed into my pack earlier. Fortunately, it was right there on top and within a minute I was able to place the flashlight into Dave's hand.

"You wait here, Charlie," Dave told me.

I watched nervously as he knelt down and crawled into the small doorway leading back into the mine. It seemed like he was gone for a long time, but probably only ten minutes had passed before he appeared again, gasping for air and covered in coal dust.

"Jap's been caught in a cave-in back there," he announced. "There's no way we can get him out by ourselves. You're going to have to go for help, Charlie."

"Me? Why me?" I pleaded. "I don't know if I can find my way down the mountain alone. It's a long way back to town."

"I have to stay here with Jap," Dave stated firmly. "I want you to go out the door and turn right. Then keep going straight until you come to the slag dump which is a long steep slippery slope of what looks like shiny black coal. That will be the quickest way down the mountain, right down the slag dump. The slag will be a little loose under your feet and you can almost slide down it if you try," Dave quickly explained.

"When you get to the bottom, turn left along the creek and you'll find the road. Just run along the road and get help. Bring some folks back here with lights, tools and whatever they need. You will probably find several men there at the company store and they will gladly come to the aid of another miner."

Turning away from me and heading back into the mine, Dave added, "I'm depending on you, Charlie. Hurry on now and run for all you're worth. I don't know how long Jap can hang on without help."

I found the slag dump just where Dave said it would be. As I stepped out on it my foot started to sink and I sort of jumped backward and landed square on my behind. Away I went, slipping and sliding down the mountain on the slag. It was scary, but once I started down there was no way to stop. I was down that mountain in record time, slipping, sliding and tumbling head over heels all the way to the bottom.

Without even stopping to catch my breath, I ran down the road toward town. Just as Dave had predicted, there were a number of men having coffee together in the company store. I guess when I walked in the door, I probably looked more like the "tar baby" from an Uncle Remus tale than an eight year old white boy. I was breathing really hard with sweat pouring out of every pore. My nose and throat were clogged with coal dust, but I managed to deliver the message that Jap Ewings was trapped in his mine and desperately in need of immediate help.

Within a very short time, ten of the men piled into a pickup truck, stopping only to pick up some tools, lights and other equipment, and we were headed up the mountain by way of the old logging road. They insisted that I go back with them since I knew exactly how to get to the old man's cabin.

Arriving at the clearing where Dave and I had camped, we were forced to leave the pickup truck because the woods were so dense. I ran along ahead of them down the narrow path. All the way they kept saying, "Hurry up, boy! Jap needs us. Hurry! Hurry!"

I ran as fast as my legs would carry me and finally we reached the cabin. They told me to wait outside and then all ten of them went back into the mine. I could hear them shouting to one another as they worked to free the old hermit.

At long last they carried Jap out of the mine and laid him on his cot. He was a pretty sad sight. The old man was covered in coal dust with his pants in shreds and blood streaming from his right leg. One of the men said that Jap's leg appeared to be broken, plus he had a pretty bad cut on his head. They proceeded to fashion a splint for his leg and to bandage his head as best they could. It was decided to keep him on his cot and just load the whole thing into the back of the pickup. So using the cot as a stretcher, they carried Jap through the woods to the truck while Dave and I brought up the rear.

With Jap's cot taking up so much of the room in the truck's bed, the men hung on to the sides as best they could for the ride down the mountain. They had saved just enough space for Dave and me to squeeze in beside the cot. I was really glad because my legs had just about given out and I ached in every bone in my body.

Once down the mountain, Dave and I were dropped off at the company store along with six of the men. The other four went with the truck and Jap over to the Layland Clinic, the nearest medical facility to Quinnimont. They promised that they would telephone us as soon as they had some word on Jap's condition.

While we waited, the store keeper gave us each a cold soda from the cooler, saying that it was free for everybody in the rescue party. I didn't think I was to be included since I never went back into the mine to help with the actual rescue.

But the store manager announced, "If it hadn't been for you, Charlie boy, and your quick trip down the mountain, old Jap may not have made it back to town in time. Why you are really the hero of the day!"

"I'm not any hero," I protested. "All I did was come to town to get these guys to go up the mountain to help Dave get Jap out of the mine."

"You sure are a hero, boy, and don't let anyone tell you any different," the storekeeper insisted.

At those words, all the people in the store gathered around me and patted me on the back. Some of the ladies even hugged me, in spite of the fact I was filthy dirty and covered from head to toe with coal dust.

We waited there at the store for nearly two hours before the phone call from the clinic finally came. Old Jap was going to be okay. Yes, he did have a broken right leg and it took ten stitches to close the wound on his head, but he was out of danger. They were going to take him to Beckley by ambulance later that evening to have the leg set and a cast put in place. The clinic was only for emergencies and didn't have an x-ray or any other such equipment.

When Dave and I finally got back to the house, Grandma took one look at us and sent us to the creek with a bar of soap and some clean clothes. I had one quick look at myself in the mirror and was shocked to see a black boy looking back at me. I had coal dust covering me from top to bottom and Dave didn't look any better. In fact, maybe he looked even worse because he had spent a lot of time with Jap in the mine before the rescue party arrived.

That night Dave and I had to retell our whole camping adventure to Grandpa and Tommy when they came home from work. Grandpa said that he was sure glad my folks had allowed me to stay on in Quinnimont for a couple of extra days. If our camping trip hadn't taken place, probably no one would have found old Jap for a long time. He would have just died there all alone trapped in his own coal mine. We had come along at just the right time. Grandpa actually called it a miracle!

"What's going to happen to Jap now?" I asked Grandpa.

"Well, he certainly can't go back up the mountain until that leg is mended. In the meantime, I guess he'll have to take a bed at the boarding house here in Quinnimont. The Widow Breeden will take good care of him and make sure he's well fed.

"But how will he pay for his room and his meals?" I wondered aloud.

"Jap actually has a good bit of money," Grandpa replied. "He just doesn't like spending it unless he actually has to. His family made a lot of money from coal when they had their mines working. Old Jap seems to like the life of a hermit. He prefers to live alone up there on the mountain where nobody bothers him. When he's all healed up, you can rest assured he'll be making his way back up the mountain. That's where he's really happy."

That night I went to bed shortly after dinner was over. The last thing I can remember before falling asleep was that I included old Jap among the people I asked God to bless in my prayers. I don't know if I even said "amen" at the end of the prayer, but I'm sure the Lord didn't mind. He knew how really tired I was. It had been a long hard day.

CHAPTER 18

A Call to Action

It was two days before Dr. LeHue was finally able to complete a call to the Billows residence. The phone was answered by Archie Billows who bellowed out in a gruff raspy voice, "Hello!"

"Is this the Alvin Billows residence?" asked Dr. LeHue politely.

"Yep, it sure is. But Alvin ain't home. He's been gone for a few days and I'm not sure exactly when he'll be coming back."

Dr. LeHue paused before continuing. "I'm very sorry to say that I'm calling with some bad news. Mr. Billows has been involved in a serious motorcycle accident near Lewisburg, West Virginia."

"Alvin's done been mixed up in a motorcycle accident, you say?"

"That's right, and his condition is listed as critical. I'm Dr. William LeHue, his attending physician. With whom am I speaking?"

"My name is Archie, Alvin's brother, his older brother.

"Is his father or mother available to come to the phone?"

"Well, Poppa passed on a few years back and Mamma ain't here right now. I don't rightly know when she'll be home."

"You say that you're Alvin's older brother?"

"Yep, by two years. There are four of us. Abner is the oldest and Alex the youngest. Alvin is between me and Alex."

"I see," said Dr. LeHue. "Then I'll just go ahead and give you the information about your brother. He's in the intensive care unit with a broken neck and a very serious brain injury. There are also numerous lacerations and bruises and I believe that his left leg is also broken. Do you have a pencil and paper there? If so, you can write down the hospital address."

There was such a long silence that Dr. LeHue thought for a moment that the connection had been broken.

Then Archie spoke up, "Naw, I ain't got no pencil and besides I don't write none too well. But I got me a really good memory, so go ahead."

"Okay, but be sure you don't forget any of this," the doctor stated. "It's important that your mother knows where her son has been hospitalized. Are you ready?"

"Sure, just let me know where Alvin is and I'll tell Momma."

Without a great deal of confidence that the message was going to be delivered, Dr. LeHue slowly spelled out the details. "He's in Ronceverte, West Virginia in the Greenbrier County Hospital. That's near Lewisburg and not far from the Virginia border. Your brother has been placed under arrest and visitors are limited to family. There is a guard by his door."

"Under arrest!" Archie shouted into the phone. "What's Alvin done this time? Was he speeding or something?"

"Well, actually the charge is a lot worse than speeding. As I understand it, your brother tried to murder some young boy and was being chased by the police at the time of the accident.

He missed a turn on a mountain road and lost control of his motorcycle."

Dr. LeHue waited a moment for Archie to reply and when there seemed to be no response coming, he continued, "He's lost a lot of blood, but his head and neck injuries are the most serious. He's presently in a coma."

At that, Archie chimed in. "A coma, you say? What's that? Are you saying that Alvin's unconscious?"

As far as the physician was concerned, this was like trying to explain something to a child. "Sometimes when the brain sustains a very hard blow, the body tends to shut down and falls into a deep sleep. I expect Alvin will wake up in another day or two, but we never really know how long a person will remain in a coma. It could be a day or it could be a week or so."

"Tell me again where Alvin is," Archie demanded. "Momma will skin me alive if I get this wrong."

Once more very patiently Dr. LeHue repeated the name of the hospital and its location.

Archie then asked, "Can we see him if we come over to Ronceverte?"

"I would expect that can be arranged. When you arrive at the hospital, just ask for me at the desk and someone will page me. I think you have pretty much all the information you need for now." Trying to end the conversation on a softer note, the doctor added, "I'm sorry to have been the one to deliver such bad news. Perhaps the next time we speak, Alvin's condition will have improved. God bless you."

After Archie hung up the phone, he stood there scratching his head trying to assimilate all the information he had been given. He wished that he could write it all down, but his schooling was very lacking to say the least.

Suddenly it occurred to him that it was really important that he tell Jasper Jenkins what had happened to Alvin. He couldn't just sit around and wait for his mother to get home. This was something that Jasper needed to hear about immediately. So quickly he left the house, hopped onto his motorcycle and rode over to the Jenkins' farm outside of town.

Jasper heard the roar of the cycle coming down the lane and came out onto the porch to greet Archie as he pulled up in front of the house. "What's the big rush? Cat step on your tail or something?"

"Naw, nothing like that," Archie replied. "But I got me a long distance call about Alvin that you sure need to hear about. No one was home at my house so I took the call and then came right over here."

"Alvin? Who in the world would be calling long distance about Alvin?" Jenkins asked.

"Some doctor in West Virginia. Alvin's been in an accident and they've got him in the hospital in a coma, whatever that is," Archie answered getting off of his bike.

"You say a doctor called you?"

"Yep, a Dr. LeHue from Ronceverte, West Virginia."

Somehow Jasper could sense that the news was going to get worse before it got better. "Did he say how the accident happened?"

"Yeah. He said that the police was chasing him and he wrecked on some mountain road over there. And the doctor said that Alvin's under arrest for murder or something really bad like that."

"Where is this hospital? Someone needs to go see him," Jasper stated emphatically. "I'm really glad you came over to tell me this, but now you need to go find your mother and brothers and let them know what happened."

As Archie got back on his motorcycle, Jasper added, "Be sure to tell Abner to come over here as soon as he can. I need to talk to him right away."

As he watched Archie ride away, Jenkins stood there on the porch pondering what his next move should be. If Alvin was to awake from the coma and start to talk, a lot of folks were going to be in serious trouble.

"Our whole scheme of things is starting to unravel," he thought. "So many things have gone wrong. There's the kid who happened to wake up and look out the window at the very moment that Alvin's hood slipped off. Then the kid completely disappears. It's been one problem after another."

Jasper made a mental list of the problems that had arisen since the night at the jail when it all started. The Bishop kid was at the top of the list. He could see now that he had made a mistake in sending Alvin to track down the missing boy. The stupid clown had really botched up that job and attracted the attention of the police. It sounded like Alvin had actually killed the kid and ended up in a hospital somewhere in the hills of West Virginia under arrest for murder. Who knew what Alvin was going to say when he came out of the coma? He could implicate them all. The whole situation was a disaster.

"I guess I best get some of the guys together and formulate a plan so that we don't all get involved. That would really be bad," he thought to himself. "I need to call a meeting to talk to everyone."

Jasper didn't want to draw any more attention than necessary to himself so he decided to have those involved meet at his deer camp up on the mountain. No one ever went up there at this time of year and they could talk openly about the situation without fear of anyone overhearing or even knowing that they were meeting. His camp was where the group had met on the night of the lynching. It was private and out of the way, the perfect spot for the clandestine meeting.

Having made his decision, Jasper got into his pickup truck and drove into town to spread the news of the meeting to a couple of the men. If each fellow he informed of the meeting would tell one or two others, it would be a good way to get the word around to everyone quickly. No phone calls would have to be made and there would be no undue suspicion aroused because of him talking personally with each individual.

When his task was accomplished, Jasper headed up the mountain to the deer camp, his mind flooded with possible plans as to how the problem of Alvin could be permanently solved.

Meanwhile, Archie Billows spotted his mother talking to a friend outside of the A&P store as he rode back through town. He pulled up in front of the grocery, hopped off his motorcycle and informed her right there on the sidewalk all about Alvin's accident. Archie included all the details that he could remember from the doctor's phone call and even mentioned to her that he had just come from Jasper Jenkins' house.

His mother's friend just happened to be the wife of a deputy sheriff and she listened intently to everything that Archie was sharing with his mother. The friend, Ethel Goodman, went directly from the grocery store to the sheriff's office and related to her husband everything she had overheard Archie telling his mother

The information was quickly passed on to the state police officers who were still in town investigating the lynching. They quickly realized that all of this had to be tied in some way to the lynching incident and immediately set up a surveillance scheme. They were especially interested in the fact that Archie had been to see Jasper Jenkins who was one of their prime suspects. Something was definitely afoot and they needed to be aware of what was happening.

And then through an amazing stroke of good luck, an off-duty policeman having a cup of coffee at the local cafe, just happened to hear a conversation between two men at the adjacent table. Their heads were close together and they were whispering something about a secret meeting that was going to be held that night at Jasper's hunting camp up on the mountain. It was the break the police had been praying would come along. Not only would the entire Jenkins' gang be at the meeting, but the police were also now planning to attend.

CHAPTER 19

The Meeting

As darkness began to fall in the mountains of western Virginia that evening, a number of law enforcement officers were concealed in the bushes along the lane leading to the Jasper Jenkins' hunting camp. Their instructions were to attempt to identify everyone who was attending the meeting and to get the license numbers of their vehicles. However, they were not to show themselves or make any arrests.

Between the hours of seven and eight o'clock, eight vehicles arrived at the camp. As best the police could discern, there were approximately fifteen men who were attending the meeting. One car arrived a little later than the others and pulled into the parking area. Two guys finally got out and walked over to the cabin carrying what appeared to be two cases of beer. Through the windows, the police could observe the men having a rousing good time, slapping each other on the back and doing a lot of laughing. It sounded more like a party than a secret meeting.

When it was totally dark, Chief Dinkins and one other local policeman cautiously crept up to opposite sides of the cabin in order to get a better look through the windows and to identify as many of the men as possible. Jasper Jenkins, who seemed to be in charge of the gathering, was observed standing in front of the pot-bellied stove and was obviously trying to quiet the group down. It looked like party time was over and they were ready to get to the serious business of the night.

As they peeked through the windows, the two policemen looked very closely at each person in the room attempting to put names on the familiar faces of the participants. When they finally retreated back to the outlying bushes and compared their lists, they had come up with fifteen names.

At the top of both of their lists was Jasper Jenkins.

Then there were the three Billows boys: Abner, Archie and Alex;

Joe Falkner, the dad of Frances Falkner, the girl who had been raped; Frances' uncle, Reggie Falkner;

Clarence Cogbill, the postal clerk;

Harry Spears, a local farmer;

George Hampton and Luke Langer, both currently unemployed;

Mike Jones, the plumber;

Stumpy Jones, Mike's cousin;

Bobby Lee, named after Robert E. Lee, the famous general;

Muley Smith, called "Muley" because he was so stubborn;

And last but not least, Alfred Stone, an auto mechanic.

There were also two additional men that the policemen didn't recognize, giving a grand total of seventeen men attending the meeting.

All of the officers strained from their surveillance spots to make out what was being discussed at the meeting. It was amazing how much they were able to hear and what they overheard astounded them. But it also confirmed much of what the police had already suspected.

After Jasper Jenkins finally got the men quiet, he related to them about Alvin's accident, giving all the details about his injuries. He especially emphasized the fact that Alvin was in a coma and had not regained consciousness since the motorcycle wreck. Jasper made it very clear that Alvin had been placed under arrest and that a guard was stationed outside of his hospital room.

Someone in the rear of the cabin shouted out, "What if Alvin wakes up and talks? Is he going to tell them about everyone involved in the lynching? We could all be arrested and thrown into jail. What was Alvin doing in West Virginia anyway?"

Jasper held up his hand to quiet the men as they began to murmur among themselves. "Hold on just a minute! Alvin was in West Virginia because I sent him there. I'm sure you haven't forgotten that Alvin's hood slipped off at the jail and some kid saw him from the window of the house across the street."

Several nodded their heads as they recalled the incident.

"We think that the boy who saw Alvin is Rob Bishop's youngest son, Charlie, who was staying at the Frank's house that night. The kid seems to be the only link that the cops have to any of us," Jasper explained, trying to keep his voice calm and his hands from shaking. "Apparently his folks sent him to stay with his grandparents in a little town called Quinnimont in West Virginia. I think they were afraid that Alvin had recognized him."

Pointing his finger in the direction of Clarence Cogbill, he continued to speak. "Our good friend here spotted a letter at the post office addressed to the Bishops from Quinnimont, so I sent Alvin there to make certain that it was the same boy who had witnessed the jailbreak."

Shaking his head in utter unbelief, Jasper remarked, "Would you believe that while Alvin was there scouting out the town, some policeman saw him and began to ask questions? Talk about dumb luck!"

131

"Well, when Alvin got back here and told me what happened, I ordered him to go back, find the kid, and make sure that he never talked to anyone. Obviously Alvin must have located the boy and taken a shot at him because it appears that he's been charged with attempted murder."

Throwing up his hands in despair, Jasper added, "I don't really know if the boy's dead or alive. I haven't heard anything about the kid and I think that if he was dead, the news would be all over town by now. But whatever, Alvin really blew it! Leave it up to a dunce like Alvin to blotch up the job."

Suddenly Abner Billows jumped to his feet. "Hey, man! That's my baby brother you're talking about," he shouted. "He ain't no dunce and don't you go calling him one neither!"

"Hold on there, Abner," Jasper responded quickly. "I didn't mean that Alvin is stupid. I just used that word because it seems like Alvin may have missed the shot. I'm guessing that the boy could still be walking around somewhere just waiting to be called to the witness stand to identify Alvin. But right now our problem ain't really the boy. Our problem is Alvin who can identify every one of us if he wakes up."

His words seemed to calm everyone down. "The last thing we need is to start fighting among ourselves. We start that and the law will break this thing wide open and we'll all find ourselves in the same jail we took those colored guys out of. I called this meeting so we can figure out how to get out of this mess that we're in right now."

"Yeah, you're right," responded Mike Jones, the plumber. "We have to stick together or we'll all be in hot water. Listen to Jasper. He's the brains of this outfit. Didn't he plan the breakout and the lynching? Look how well those things came off."

"Thanks Mike!" Jasper answered. "Now listen, we all came here tonight to make some plans. First, we have to consider the fact that Alvin just might wake up and start telling the cops everything. And secondly, we have to figure out what to do about this Bishop kid. Do we still need to shut him up or can we just forget about the boy and concentrate on Alvin?"

No one said a word. Jasper spoke into the silence and demanded, "Come on guys! Give me some feedback. You can't expect me to do all the thinking, can you?"

"That's right, Jasper," piped in George Hampton. "All our necks could be in a noose if we don't stick together."

Then Clarence Cogbill threw in his two cents. "I believe we need a plan for both Alvin and the kid. If Alvin wakes up and begins to sing, we will have to plug up his mouth or, like Mike just said, we'll all be in a heap of trouble. So let's consider Alvin first and then the kid."

Clarence obviously had everyone's attention, so he continued to share his idea. "The Bishop boy can only lead the cops to one person and that's Alvin. So Alvin has to be our first target. I don't mean a target to shoot at necessarily, but that could be the solution. After all, we have to think of all of us and not just one guy."

"You're certainly right on that point, Clarence," said Jasper. "So let's put the kid on the back burner for the time being and concentrate on what we're going to do about Alvin. Come on, let me hear your thoughts."

Clarence sat down, and before anyone else could even open his mouth to get a word in edgewise, Jasper started talking again.

"Now you Billows boys might not like me saying this, but Alvin is just one person and we do have to think about the whole bunch of us. If he starts telling what he knows, we'll all be arrested and held responsible for lynching those three guys. We may say that what we did that night was justice, but the law says what we did was murder. No two ways about it."

Jasper paused dramatically in his tirade, but everyone just sat in stony silence considering his words. "Listen, most of you guys got a wife and kids to think about. Don't forget that we did what we did for Joe Falkner and his family and for Frances in particular to preserve her honor."

The men were all nodding their heads in agreement. "So anyway, it's possible that Alvin might not recover. He could die before he ever wakes up and everything will be covered if he does. It's not that I want Alvin dead, but he could die. Folks do die when they break their necks, you know," Jasper stated firmly.

And then Clarence was on his feet again. "But if Alvin wakes up, we need to be there and be sure that he doesn't give us all away. Or considering what he knows, maybe we need to be sure that he doesn't wake up. We can't take any chances. We need to take action now."

Slowly looking around the room, Clarence added these final words. "I've had my say. I'm finished. Or maybe I should say that we're all finished if Alvin ever wakes up."

Jasper took control of the meeting again and asked, "Does anyone else have anything that they want to say?"

After a short silence, Abner Billows stood to his feet and spoke up. "I guess the lot sort of falls to me. After all, I'm Alvin's oldest brother and the head of our family, so I suppose it's really my duty to handle this situation and I'm going to stand by that. If you all want, I'll go on down to this Ronceverte place and check out just exactly what's going on there at the hospital. But I ain't got no money to make the trip, so you guys will have to help me out with that."

"But what will you do if Alvin wakes up and begins to point his finger at us?" asked Reggie Falkner. "Can you possibly kill your own brother? Or perhaps the bigger question is, will you?"

"You all know that I love Alvin even though we don't get along none the best all the time. After all he is my kid brother," Abner stated. "But we're in this here mess now because of him and I guess I owe you guys something, so I'll keep him quiet, even if it means I have to shut him up for good. I remember hearing the preacher tell once at church about how somebody named Cain killed his brother Abel. If it's in the Bible about killing your brother, then it must be okay. So if I have to do it, I'll do it."

Abner actually choked up a little and had to stop for a minute to regain his composure. But he finally got hold of himself and went on. "I'm not really sure Alvin would want to go on living anyway with his brains all scrambled up. And maybe his broken leg ain't going to get no better and he couldn't walk or ride his motorcycle no more. Alvin would probably be a lot better off in heaven with Poppa and the angels. And if he's in heaven, none of us would ever have to go to some prison for the rest of our lives."

Suddenly Abner turned back again to the practical side of things. "I don't own no pistol so one of you guys are gonna have to give me a gun to use if I need it. Plus, everyone's gonna to have to kick in some cash to cover the trip. Remember that I might have to stay in West Virginia for more than one night, so open up your wallets and give me some hard cash."

Then Jasper was on his feet again. "It's seems to be all settled then. Abner says that he's our man for the job. That's good enough for me. Now I'm going to put my cap on the table and I expect you guys to cough up as much cash as you got on you. Abner is going to need money for gas, food and a place to stay while he's there in Ronceverte. I'll arrange for the gun."

With that everyone began to dig into their pockets and make their way to the table to fill the cap that was sitting there.

Sensing that the meeting was about to break up, the police officers who were listening outside of the house, quietly slipped back into the woods and joined the other lawmen that were hiding there. When everyone who attended the meeting in the cabin had finally departed, the police slowly made their way back into town and gathered at the police station to consider how to act upon all they had heard.

It felt good to have the upper hand and to be working on the solution before the problem even became a reality.

Chapter 20

The Switcheroo

The following morning the police were hard at work organizing the evidence they had accumulated during their investigation. Backed by the intelligence they had gathered the night before when the meeting was held at Jenkins' deer camp, they now had a solid list of some fifteen names of people who had been actively involved in the lynching. The Commonwealth of Virginia had sent over three senior detectives, who were accompanied by two attorneys from the state attorney general's office, to begin putting a case together against those who had carried out the heinous crime.

One of the first things that the attorneys did was to secure a warrant for a wire tap on Jasper Jenkins' telephone line from one of the judges of the Stuart County Court. Upon receiving the necessary permission, the tap was immediately placed upon the phone and manned by the detectives around the clock.

For the first few days that the tap was in place, there were no calls of interest. The detectives sat hour after hour wearing their headphones, waiting for someone to contact Jasper. Finally, on the fifth day about four o'clock in the afternoon, a long distance call was picked up from Ronceverte, West Virginia coming from none other than Abner Billows. It was the payoff for which the detectives had been waiting.

"Hello, Jasper. This is Abner and I'm here in West Virginia."

"Good to hear your voice. I was wondering when you were going to call. What's the news?" Jasper asked impatiently.

"Well, apparently Alvin began to wake up a bit this afternoon. At least that's what the doctor told me a few minutes ago."

"What did the doctor say?" Jasper asked, feeling panic start to rise within him. "Did Alvin say anything damaging or name any names?"

"The doctor didn't tell me if he said anything only that he had opened his eyes and was starting to stir around a little. I don't think he's come out of the coma all the way yet," Abner responded.

"Stay close. If Alvin begins to run his mouth, you're going to have to shut him up quick," Jasper continued. "Can you do that, Abner? Everyone here is counting on you."

"I told you that I'd take care of it," Abner stated firmly. "I've got this here gun you give me stuck in my belt and I'm ready to use it if I have to."

"What about the guard?" Jasper inquired. "Is there still a policeman outside the door?"

"Yeah, there's always someone there by the door, but that ain't no problem," Abner assured him. "They let me go in whenever I want to see him. Actually I think the guards sort of like me."

"How much longer before he starts talking, do you think?" Jasper was really pushing for an answer to the big question. "We can't take any chances."

"Well, according to what the doctor told me earlier, it could be another twenty-four hours or so until he's really awake, so ain't no real rush," Abner said confidently. "Relax. I've got everything under control."

And then Abner proceeded to share the plan he had devised.

"Alvin's room is right on the ground floor in the back of the building, So all I really have to do to make my move is just wait 'til around midnight when the hospital is sort of closed down for the night. My bike will be hid round back in the bushes and then all I have to do is sneak up to Alvin's window and it's all over with just one shot."

Abner paused for a moment and then added, "And would you believe that Alvin's bed is right next to the window? There ain't no way that I can miss. I can fire the gun and be away in two minutes flat."

Listening to him, Jasper had to admit that Abner had it all worked out. "What's your escape plan?" he asked.

"I got that all worked out too," Abner replied. "The hospital is south of town close to the highway. When the police realize what happened, they would probably expect that whoever shot Alvin would use the main road and go up the mountain to Lewisburg and then head east toward Virginia. But instead I'm gonna cross the bridge over the river and go south on US 219. Then just a couple of miles further on I found a small road that goes northeast and connects to US 60 about ten miles from the Virginia line. I'll be in Covington before the police can even start looking for me."

Jasper had to acknowledge that the escape route that Alvin had outlined was the work of a genius. It really seemed like he could pull the whole thing off and get away scot-free.

"Well Abner, you certainly know the lay of the land better than I do. I've never even been down there. It sure sounds like a good solid plan to me," Jasper told him. "Just don't lose your nerve. Do what you have to do and then get back here."

"Don't worry, you can count on me," Abner said with assurance. "I'll be glad to have this over with and get away from this two-bit town."

It sounded like the conversation was over, but then Abner thought of one more thing. "Give Momma a call and tell her I'm comin' home. She always worries about me when I'm away."

"No problem. I guess we've covered everything. See you tomorrow." And with those words, Jasper hung up the phone.

The Virginia police listening in on the conversation could hardly believe their ears. They had not only heard Abner's plans to kill his own brother, but his escape plan as well. When they gave their report to those in charge of the investigation, counter plans were immediately formulated.

First, the guards at the hospital were cautioned to be very careful when Abner was around. Then Dr. LeHue was contacted and informed about the plot to murder Alvin Billows in his bed before he regained consciousness and was able to be questioned by the police.

The doctor suggested that perhaps Alvin could be moved secretly to the second floor of the hospital and some sort of dummy placed in his first floor bed. The officers really liked the doctor's idea and decided to carry it out as soon as possible. They just needed to be sure that Abner, who was spending most of his time in the waiting room, didn't come walking down the hall while they were making the transfer. Secret preparations were made to assure that the plan would run smoothly.

It was around eight o'clock when the doctor paid a visit to Alvin's room, supposedly to take a final look at his patient before going home for the night. Visiting hours were just coming to an end and the hospital doors were all being locked up. Only the emergency room door could be used during the nighttime hours.

Abner was outside of Alvin's room talking to the guard when Dr. LeHue completed his examination and the physician asked him if he could step into his office for a few minutes.

"This won't take long," he explained to Abner, "but I do want to update you on your brother's condition so you know what to expect."

Abner was eager to hear what the doctor had to say and eagerly followed him down the long hall to his office near the main entrance.

"Come in and sit down," Dr. LeHue said. "This won't take too long. The news is very good. Your brother is opening his eyes occasionally and is even starting to move his arms and good leg. He isn't out of the coma yet, but he seems to be gradually showing definite signs of improvement."

Reaching out and putting his hand on Abner's shoulder, he said, "I fully expect that he should be responsive and even talking sometime around nine o'clock in the morning. In fact, I put a call in to the police while I was just in Alvin's room about the promising signs I am seeing and they told me they will be here first thing in the morning to talk with him."

Dr. LeHue smiled broadly at Abner. "You will probably want to be here first thing in the morning too, so you'll have a few minutes to spend with your brother before the police arrive."

Picking up his hat from the corner of his desk, Dr. LeHue said, "Come on. We can walk out to the front door together because visiting hours ended a few minutes ago and I can let you out."

Abner had no choice but to follow the physician out of the hospital and into the parking lot where they shook hands and the doctor got into his car and drove away.

Little did Abner know that while he had been in the doctor's office, Alvin had been taken upstairs to another room along with a second guard. In Alvin's former room, his bed had been arranged in such a way that it appeared to anyone glancing into the darkened room that Alvin was still there sleeping peacefully by the window with his usual guard stationed outside the door. The police had worked quickly and everything was in place. The scene was set.

And as far as Abner was concerned, everything was working out perfectly for his plan to be put into action. Alvin was still in the coma, so he hadn't been able to reveal anything to the police. The hospital was closed down tight for the night with only a small staff on duty. The parking lot was empty. It was perfect. Abner decided to stick with his plan to wait until midnight, so he walked down the street and into a beer joint to pass the next few hours.

The area around the hospital appeared deserted when Abner returned. He was surprised how dark it was, but Abner had never had any trouble seeing in the dark. Quickly he made his way to the rear of the building and found the window to Alvin's room.

As he peeked into the room, he could clearly see what he thought was his younger brother lying in the bed right next to the window. Using his knife, Abner cut the screen covering the window and then pulled the pistol from his belt. He took careful aim and then fired three quick shots into what he was convinced was his brother's head. One, two, three! Then immediately Abner ran to the bushes, jumped on his motorcycle and sped away. It had been far easier than he had even imagined. He just pulled the trigger and it was done. It was like no one even realized that it happened. He had pulled it off like a professional hit man. Alvin was never going to talk to anyone ever again.

Of course, Abner never suspected for a minute that the police had outsmarted him. Being forewarned of Abner's escape route, the police had decided to trap him when he crossed the bridge rather than on the highway or a city street. They had men hidden at both ends of the narrow bridge awaiting his arrival.

142

Just as Abner came onto the bridge, police cars pulled out and blocked both ends of the bridge. It only took Abner a second to realize that he was trapped with no way of escape. Rather than putting up any resistance, he slammed on his brakes and skidded to a stop right in the middle of the bridge. Then he pulled out his pistol, threw it into the river and raised his hands in surrender.

It was all over. The police had their man.

CHAPTER 21

The Visitation

During the night Alvin Billows did come out of his coma and the policeman guarding him quickly summoned a physician to the room. As soon as the doctor leaned over his patient, Alvin looked up at him and said, "I need to see a preacher. I got something important that I need to tell him right now."

"You want a preacher?" Dr. LeHue asked, a bit startled by the sudden request coming from the man on the bed.

"Yep, there's something that I can only tell a preacher man and I need him to come as quick as he can," Alvin stated in a voice amazingly strong for someone in his weakened condition.

Dr. LeHue turned to the nurse at his side and requested that she call a pastor from one of the local churches to come to the hospital as quickly as possible.

After a moment's thought, she replied, "I'll call Pastor Stellman from the Baptist Church. He lives just a block or two away and I know him personally. I'm sure that he'll be willing to come."

While she was making the call, the doctor examined Alvin, taking his pulse and blood pressure and other vital signs and was pleased to find him in a greatly improved condition. In fact, he was amazed at how well Alvin was doing considering the extent of his injuries.

In less than twenty minutes, Reverend Stellman arrived at Alvin's bedside. Pulling a chair up beside the bed, the pastor reached out and took the hand of the man who lay there swaddled in layers of bandages. Although he had never seen him before, Pastor Stellman was moved with deep compassion.

"Hello there," he said quietly. "I'm Pastor Stellman from First Baptist Church here in Ronceverte. I understand you told the doctor that you needed to talk to a minister. Is that correct?"

"Yep, it sure is. You is a preacher, ain't you?" Alvin stammered.

"That's right. I'm duly ordained to minister the gospel by the Southern Baptist Convention. How can I help you, son?"

"I seen the Lord!" Alvin exclaimed. "He come to me as clear as I see you right now. He said I must confess my sins and I got a whole bunch of them that I need to unload."

The pastor didn't quite know how to reply to Alvin's astonishing statement. "You say you actually saw the Lord?"

"Yep! He stood right over there," Alvin said pointing in the general direction of the door. "He looked down on me with such a warm, loving smile and called me Alvin. He done called me by name! The Lord knowed my name!"

Alvin paused in his testimony, as though he were caught up in the remembrance of the encounter, before continuing.

"Then the Lord said to me, 'Your sin stands between you and eternal life. You must cleanse your soul.' And then He was gone. He just vanished. But I knowed that Jesus came to me and told me what I gotta do and so that's why I called for you. I know I gotta do it and I gotta do it now!"

"It certainly sounds as though you have had a real visitation from the Lord Jesus. What is it that you need to tell me?" the minister asked.

"Well, I best start at the beginning. Back in Lee's Junction where I live, these three colored guys raped a white girl that I knowed. The police arrested them and put them in jail, but my friend Jasper Jenkins said we shouldn't just sit around and wait for a trial. So late one night, a bunch of us guys took our guns, put on hoods and busted into the jail. We grabbed them rapists and took them out to the hill west of town and strung them up. Then it was like we went crazy and we starting shootin' at them hanging there."

The pastor wasn't exactly sure what to say, but he interrupted Alvin and asked, "Are you telling me that you were part of a lynch mob?"

"Yes sir, I was. I truly thought it was the right thing to do at the time, you know. I was right upset about what had happened and so was everyone else," Alvin explained. "But that ain't all. There was this kid what looked out his window and he seen me out there on the street just when my hood slipped off. Looked right into my eyes, he did. He knowed me as sure as the night is dark. I knowed his face, but not his name."

Tears began to run down Alvin's face as he recounted the events that had taken place.

"I told Jasper about the boy in the window the next day and we went searching for the kid, but couldn't find him anywhere. And then someone, I ain't sure who, got the idea that he might be hiding out in a little hick town in West Virginia called Quinnimont, so I went there looking for him. But would you believe that someone wearing a badge ran me plum out of town?"

All the pastor had time to do was nod his head before Alvin continued on with his confession. It was like once Alvin started talking, he couldn't stop until he came to the bitter end.

"But I went back there again because I was sure the boy was holed up there someplace. And I found him and, I'm right sorry to have to tell you this, but I shot him. I actually shot that little kid right through the window as he was sitting there at the table eating his supper."

By this time Alvin was weeping and the pastor pulled a handkerchief out of his pocket and put it in Alvin's hand. "And then what happened?" he prompted.

"I just took off. I got on my bike and rode like the wind out of town. Some police car began to chase me as I started down this here mountain. I was going so fast that I missed a turn and went flying off the road into the brush. I remember crying out, 'Jesus, save me!' and that's all I recollect until Jesus came to me tonight. Will God ever forgive me, Preacher?" Alvin asked through his tears.

"Well son, I must say that is really some story," Pastor Stellman responded. "But I know that the Lord Jesus forgives sinners. In the Bible it tells us that if we confess our sins, He is faithful and just to forgive us our sins and to cleanse us from all unrighteousness. That's what it says in First John, chapter one."

The pastor reached out and took hold of Alvin's hand and told him, "You've made your confession and I am convinced that your sins are forgiven."

In a relieved voice, Alvin said, "You really feel I done been forgiven? I ain't gonna go to hell?"

Pastor Stellman had to smile a little as he replied, "You may go to jail, Alvin, but you won't go to hell. The Lord has forgiven you and opened the door to heaven. Probably you'll be recalling some other things you'll want to confess to the Lord in the days and weeks ahead," he continued, "and if that happens, you can just open your heart and talk to the Lord."

Glancing down at the bedridden man, the pastor could sense the peace that had come over him. "If you would like, I'll be happy to come and visit with you while you're here in the hospital."

"Yeah, I'd like that," Alvin replied still holding tightly to his hand.

"One more thing before I leave tonight," Pastor Stellman added. "I'd like for you to follow me in a short prayer. I think it will really seal your salvation. Will you pray with me?"

"Yup, I'll do just that." Almost automatically, Alvin bowed his head.

"Just repeat these words after me," the pastor told him. "Lord Jesus, I'm a sinner. I'm sorry for all my sins that I just confessed and for all my other sins too. Please forgive me and cleanse me of all my sin. I open my heart and ask you to come in and be my Lord and my Savior. Thank You, Jesus!"

Alvin dutifully followed every word, repeating them as Pastor Stellman led him through the prayer.

Finally standing up as he prepared to leave, the pastor suggested to Alvin that he might want to speak with the police and also tell them the same things he had just confessed to the Lord.

"You need to clear your conscience and own up to everything that has happened," he told Alvin. "It won't be easy, but you can't have real peace until you bring this out into the open."

"Yeah," Alvin agreed, "that would probably be the right thing to do. Will you tell them that for me?"

Both the guard and the nurse, who had been in the room the entire time, had tears in their eyes as the pastor left. Alvin just seemed to relax and quickly fell into a restful sleep.

The next morning after eating a light breakfast, Alvin was visited by the West Virginia state's attorney for Greenbrier

County, Charles Greer, who introduced himself and sat down in the chair next to the bed. "I understand there is something that you want to talk to me about, is that correct?" he asked.

"Yes sir," Alvin replied. "That preacher fellow what come last night, he really helped me confess my sins to Jesus. But before he left, he told me that I needed to confess everything to you lawmen too. So I guess that's why you're here right now."

"Do you understand what it means to make a confession?" Mr. Greer inquired, making sure that Alvin knew exactly what he would be doing as they talked together.

"Yep, I sure do," Alvin confirmed. "There's a lot inside of me that I need to get out about everything that's happened this summer."

The attorney was somewhat surprised at how eager Alvin was to confess, but arrangements were quickly made to get someone to come to the hospital to take down his statement.

It was only a short time later when a woman arrived with a steno machine and took her place at a small table. Mr. Greer explained to Alvin in great detail how every word he said would be taken down, transcribed and then typed up. All Alvin would have to do is sign the document when it was completed.

Alvin sort of smirked and said that it was a lot easier to confess to Jesus than to the court people.

During the next half hour or so Alvin made a full and complete confession as to his part in removing the colored boys from the jail in Lee's Junction and the subsequent lynching that took place on the hill. He named as many of the men who were involved in the lynching as he could remember. He also confessed to tracking down the Bishop kid in Quinnimont and firing a shot at him through the window. Alvin ended his summary of the events by relating how he had cried out to the Lord before crashing into the thicket on the mountainside.

The stenographer took down every word that Alvin said. Before leaving the room to return to her office, she advised Mr. Greer that it would take her a few hours to transcribe the statement, but that she should have the document completed before two o'clock that afternoon. Making the confession had really exhausted Alvin, but he was glad he had done it and he certainly felt a lot better on the inside.

"Ill notify the authorities in Fayette County and also those in Virginia and make them aware that you have confessed to these various crimes," the attorney informed him.

There was one big question that was still bugging Alvin. He had to know the answer. "Mr. Greer, am I gonna go to jail?" he asked with trepidation.

"That's not for me to say," the lawyer replied. "If you actually killed the Bishop kid, as you called him, you will certainly have to stand trial for that. But it will be up to the judge and jury to determine how long you would have to serve in prison."

Mr. Greer paused for a minute or two before continuing. "What's the name of the place where you shot the little boy? I need to know so I can check around and find out exactly what happened."

"It was in some little place called Quinnimont right here in West Virginia," Alvin responded. "He was just sitting there at the table eating his supper when I pulled the trigger. The poor little kid didn't even know I was a-gunnin' for him. I feel really bad about what I done, but I guess there's no way I can undo it now. What's done is done."

The attorney looked over at Alvin all bandaged up there on the bed and really felt sorry for him. "Well, Alvin, I'll see what information is available and I'll get back to you. Meanwhile, you realize that you are under arrest here in the hospital and will have to appear before a judge just as soon as you are deemed strong enough to testify."

"Do you think that I can have some of my folks come here to visit me?" Alvin asked.

"Well, certainly not your brother, Abner. I guess you know he's being held in the county jail for attempted murder," Mr. Greer replied.

"Murder? Who did Abner try to kill?"

"You don't know?" the attorney asked incredulously.

"No sir, I ain't got no idea. Abner ain't one to just go around killing people. I can't imagine who he'd want to kill. That's crazy!"

"Alvin, I'm really sorry to have to be the one to tell you this, but Abner actually tried to kill you."

Alvin sat straight up in bed. "Me? My own brother tried to kill me?"

"That's right. Last night the police learned that your brother planned to shoot you through the window by your bed right here in the hospital. When they were informed, you were moved upstairs to this room. Don't you remember being moved up here last night?" Mr. Greer inquired. "Your brother actually slipped up outside of your old room, cut through the screen and fired three shots at what he thought was you lying there asleep on the bed." The lawyer shook his head in unbelief. "But you see, a dummy had been brought in and put under the blanket to look like you. If you had actually been in that bed, you wouldn't be here today."

Alvin's eyes were wide open in utter unbelief. "You mean my brother really thought he was killin' me?"

"What can I say?" Mr. Greer sadly replied. "Those are the facts of the situation. Abner attempted to escape, but since the police were aware of his plans, including the escape route, they caught him before he even got two miles from here.'

"Wow!" Alvin exclaimed. "The good Lord musta been lookin' out for me, don't you think?"

"Yes, I believe he was," Mrs. Greer agreed. "Now you really need to lie down there and get some rest. You've just had a real emotional shock and I think it's left you pretty exhausted."

Giving Alvin a pat on the shoulder and standing up, he said, "I'll be back with your confession as soon as it's typed up. I'll be bringing along a couple of folks to watch you sign it so that everything will be legal."

True to his word, Mr. Greer returned a few hours later with Dr. LeHue and two nurses who witnessed Alvin signing his confession and then added their signatures as witnesses. Copies of the document were forwarded to the interested parties in both West Virginia and Virginia.

CHAPTER 22

Going Home

The authorities in West Virginia were quick to phone their counterparts in Lee's Junction to tell them about Alvin Billows' confession and Abner Billows' arrest. While on the phone, they read off the names of those involved in the lynching that had been given by Alvin in his confession. The chief of police in Virginia asked if it would be possible to have copies of the confession sent to them by courier as they were anxious to round up the perpetrators as quickly as possible, so a courier was dispatched with the documents before the end of the day.

As soon as the copies of Alvin's confession arrived in Lee's Junction, the team handling the case took them over to the county judge who had been assigned to the case and requested warrants for the arrest of all those mentioned in the confession as well as any other suspects on their list of possible accomplices.

A call was sent out for additional policemen from both the State Police and the County Sheriff's Office. Teams were then formed and dispatched to apprehend all those for whom warrants had been issued. Within a very short time, all fifteen men suspected of being involved in the lynching were in custody. They were immediately photographed, fingerprinted and crowded into the four cells in the Stuart County Jail located in Lee's Junction. The county judge then set an arraignment hearing for the morning of Friday, August 22nd in the County Court House.

The authorities quickly realized that they couldn't safely keep all fifteen prisoners in the small facility available in Stuart County, so arrangements were made to transfer the majority of them to jails in three other neighboring counties. By the end of the day only four men remained incarcerated in Lee's Junction and the police were breathing a lot easier once the suspects had all been separated.

News of the arrests spread quickly and newspapers and radio stations throughout the region dispatched reporters to cover this event. The little town of Lee's Junction was ablaze with the news and rumors were flying everywhere. There hadn't been such excitement in years.

At the arraignment hearing, the judge bound all fifteen men over for trial, instructing that they were to be held without bond. The prisoners were also informed that a trial date would be set in the very near future and that they needed to procure the best legal council possible because they were facing some very serious charges.

The judge further advised the fifteen accused that the Billows' brothers, Abner and Alvin, were to be arraigned in absentee and would be extradited from West Virginia to face the charges pending against them in Virginia. The prisoners were not allowed to make any statements before being transported back to their respective jails.

Rob Bishop, Charlie's father, was on the phone to Quinnimont as soon as he had the official word to inform his in-laws that it was now safe to send Charlie back home.

"It's all over," he almost shouted into the telephone. "All told, there are seventeen men who have been arrested and we don't have to worry anymore. The police are certain that they have everyone in custody who was involved in the incident, so there's absolutely no reason that Charlie can't come back home as soon as possible. Perhaps you could even get him on the morning train tomorrow."

You could almost hear Grandpa Wilson breathe a sigh of relief. "I'm mighty glad to hear that and I know that Charlie's going to be happy when I tell him the good news. But there may be a little problem about Charlie coming home so soon. I was going to contact you about this, but I just hadn't had a chance to get word to you."

There was a pause and then Grandpa stated, "Charlie asked Jesus into his heart earlier this week and wants to be baptized in the river this Sunday afternoon. He talked to the pastor at the church and everything is all arranged. Of course, it's up to you whether he stays or not, but I think he'll be really disappointed if he misses out on this."

With some reluctance, Charlie's father agreed to the delay. "I suppose a few more days isn't going to make any difference," he finally said. "If Charlie wants to stay on, I guess it's no problem. So you say that he's actually going to be baptized in the river? I'm sorry that I'm going to miss seeing that, but I'm sure Charlie will fill me in on all the details when he gets home," he added. "Just put him on the Monday morning train to Covington and we'll be there to meet him. Perhaps Dave can make the trip with Charlie so he won't be traveling alone."

And so it was all arranged. I would be staying through the weekend in Quinnimont and then taking the train to Covington. As soon as Grandpa Wilson got home from the station later that afternoon, he shared the good news with me.

Needless to say, I was really glad to hear about the arrests and to learn that I would be soon be heading back home. "But what about my baptism on Sunday?" I asked Grandpa. "They don't baptize in the river back home and I want the kind of baptism where you go under the water."

Grandpa laughed. "Don't worry, Charlie. You're still going to be baptized. I took the matter up with your dad and he said you could stay until Monday. And he also wanted me to tell you that he wished that they could be with you for the big occasion, but that they would be thinking and praying for you on Sunday. And guess what? Dave will be going back to Covington with you on the morning train."

I was so excited that I gave my grandpa a great big hug. "Thanks, Grandpa. I'm not sure I could have talked Dad into letting me stay and I really want to be baptized."

So Sunday afternoon I walked down the well-worn path through the brush that led to the swimming hole. The pastor was standing there by the river waiting for me to arrive. The small crowd that had gathered was singing a hymn and this time I knew all the words. I was the only person who was a candidate for baptism, so it was almost like I was having my own private baptism there in the river.

As I followed the pastor into the water, I thought back over the many things that had happened during the summer while I had been in Quinnimont. I recalled the camping trip, selling candy at the minstrel show, being the batboy for the baseball team and the exciting time up on Ewings Mountain. There had been so many great adventures, but I knew beyond a shadow of a doubt that nothing would ever compare to this moment when I was publicly confessing Jesus as Lord and being baptized in the river. It was something that I would remember for the rest of my life.

The train trip homeward was uneventful. Grandpa and Grandma Bishop were waiting at the station in Hinton and came on board during the stop to greet Dave and me. Grandma Bishop had made sandwiches and cookies for us. The cookies were my favorite kind, the raisin-filled ones which she usually baked only at Christmas time.

They also brought a copy of the Charleston Gazette which had a long article about the lynching and the recent arrests of those who had been involved in the incident. The newspaper also mentioned that it was rumored that a young boy, whose name was not given, had played a major role in the identification of the men who had taken part in the lynching.

When the train started up again, the conductor, who knew both of my grandfathers, came through and spent some time talking with us and even bought us each a soda pop. During our conversation, he brought up the lynching that had occurred at Lee's Junction and asked if we knew anything about what had happened there. I think perhaps he had heard Grandpa Bishop mention that I was on my way home to Lee's Junction.

Anyway, Dave quickly tried to change the subject, but a couple across the aisle had been listening in and had a few comments of their own about the lynching incident. They ended up by asking us if we knew anything about the boy that folks were referring to as "the hero of Lee's Junction." I started to say something, but Dave elbowed me in the ribs to remind me about Grandpa's stern warning to stay away from that subject if it came up while we were on the train.

When Dave answered that we had both spent the summer in West Virginia, the couple lost interest and turned away. But I kept thinking about that word "hero" that had been used. Was I really a hero? I sure didn't think that I was any sort of hero. All I had done was to look out the window just as Alvin Billow's hood slipped off and was able to recognize him. It was only natural that I should tell the police about who it was I saw out there by the jailhouse. But the newspaper article had mentioned several times about the witness in the window. I guess people would be referring to me that way as long as there was any memory of that terrible night.

Dave and I were both standing at the top of the steps with our suitcases when the train pulled into the Covington station so we could be the first ones off. Mom, Dad and Bobby were right there waiting for us to arrive. Mom almost smothered me with kisses and I thought Dad would break my ribs with his hugs. At first Bobby stuck out his hand like he wanted to shake mine, but then he reached out and gave me a big hug and even a kiss. I guess I blushed. I had never been kissed by my brother in public.

In the car on the way home, the whole family wanted to hear all about my exciting summer. I leaned over closer to the front seat so my folks could hear what I was saying.

I hardly knew where to begin, so I started by telling them how I had starting talking to Jesus while I had been away from home. "Probably some people would call it praying, but it was really just like I was talking to Him," I informed them. "It's not like I got down on my knees or anything like that. I just sort of talked to God like I'd talk to a friend."

It was really a little hard to try to explain to my family about talking to God and all other the things that had happened over the past summer because some of my experiences were almost unbelievable. All I could do was try to bring them up to date.

"After I stayed at the Franks' house last June and saw what happened across the street at the jail, I was really scared. And then when I first got to Quinnimont, I wasn't only scared, but I was pretty homesick for a while too," I admitted. "In fact, I got so frightened when I heard that some of the bad guys were trying to track me down that I couldn't even sleep at night. I'd just lie there in bed hiding under the covers and ask the Lord to protect me and not let them find me. It was a pretty bad time."

"Your grandpa was there with you, wasn't he?" my dad asked.

"I know, but that didn't really count because he was off in another room," I said. "Anyway, I didn't want Grandpa to know how scared I really was. So like I said, I just talked to the Lord about everything and that made me feel a lot better."

Then I remembered some other things to tell them. "And of course there was the time I almost got bitten by a snake. That was pretty scary too. And worst of all was when Alvin Billows tried to shoot me while I was eating dinner. If I hadn't reached for the biscuit when I did, I'd probably be dead right now. Grandpa said it was a miracle that his bullet missed me"

I could hear my mother audibly gasp as the words continued to stumble out of my mouth. But I wasn't done yet. I still had more to tell.

"And last week on Ewings Mountain where we were camping, an old hermit got trapped in his mine and Dave had to send me down the mountain all alone to get help. I had to run through the woods all by myself and then slide down through the slag dump too. I tell you, I was terrified." My voice was probably sounding a little shaky as I tried to relate my recent experience, but I just kept going on with the story.

My parents didn't say a single word the whole time I was talking. My dad just continued driving the car and my mother had reached across the seat and was holding tightly to my hand. Bobby was just sitting there with me on the back seat with his mouth hanging open. I don't think a one of them had any idea of what had really been happening to me while I was supposedly safe from harm there in Quinnimont.

"I can tell you that I was praying really hard the whole time I was going down the mountain and I felt like God was with me every step of the way," I told them. "My heart was beating like a sledge hammer by the time I got into town and located some men to come with me to help with the rescue. Then I had to lead all ten of them back up the mountain to the cabin because I was the only one who knew where it was. But the Lord sure heard and answered my prayers because we got old Jap Ewings safely out and he's in the hospital right now."

My mother finally remarked, "We certainly need to thank God that He's been watching over you all summer."

"I do thank Him, Mom," I responded. "I thank God all the time. He's really taken good care of me. And there's something else super important that happened that I want to tell you about. I've saved the best thing until last."

I was so excited that I was finally going to be able to share with my folks about how I had come to the Lord last week. "Do you remember how I told you that Dave and I were just up on the mountain camping?" I asked. "Well anyway, the two of us got to talking about Jesus one night and about how He died on the cross. Dave ended up asking me if I had ever invited Jesus to come into my heart to be my Savior and when I told him that I had never done that, he led me in a short prayer. And guess what? Jesus actually came into my heart right there on Ewings Mountain. He forgave my sins and it was like I had a bath in love from the inside out. The pastor told me at my baptism yesterday that I had been born again."

I looked at my mom and there were big tears running down her cheeks. She may have been crying, but she looked really happy.

"That's certainly a beautiful testimony," she stammered. "I only wish your dad and I could have been there to see you baptized. But I'm sure that everything has worked out just the way the Lord planned and I must say that your summer has had a very happy ending,"

Suddenly Dad slammed on the brakes and pulled the car off of the highway. He cut off the engine, jumped out, ran around the car, opened my door and pulled me out. Then Dad gave me the biggest hug that any kid has ever received from his father.

"Son," he exclaimed, "I'm so very proud of you. I hated having you away from us for so long, but what you've just told us today has made everything fall into place. I'm so glad that you met Jesus. That's definitely the greatest experience that you'll ever have."

By this time, everyone in our family was shedding tears of joy. Even Bobby and Dave were crying. We must have spent ten minutes there on the side of the road hugging and kissing each other. I wondered later what the other folks driving along the highway that day must have thought as they passed by and saw us all rejoicing there.

CHAPTER 23

The End of Summer

It sure was good to climb into my own bed that night. I was really tried after the long trip home, but Bobby insisted on asking me all sorts of questions while I was trying to get to sleep. I don't even remember if I answered him or not.

The following morning Mom allowed me to sleep late and it must have been at least eight o'clock before I rolled out of bed and went to brush my teeth. But there was a great smell in the air that drew me to the kitchen while I was still in my pajamas. It was the smell of blueberry pancakes and real maple syrup, my favorite breakfast. I ate two whole stacks and Mom didn't even caution me to eat slower, not even once. Finally when I had pushed aside my plate, she told me that I should go and get dressed because my buddies had been calling all morning wanting to talk to me.

It was interesting how I hadn't even thought much about my hometown friends during the summer. How could I have forgotten them so easily? Of course, I had spent a lot of time hanging around with Dave and Tommy and with everything else that was going on, there hadn't been much time to think about things back home.

After I got dressed, I phoned my friends, Billy Hanson and the twins, Matthew and Mark Gillman, and arranged to meet them at our usual spot under the big pine trees in the park on Lee Street. When I arrived, they were already there waiting for me. Each one had about a hundred questions and each one of them wanted his question answered first. I eventually had to stand up and shout to get their attention.

"Come on, guys! One question at a time." But there was so much noise and confusion that I decided not to even let them ask their questions. "Hold on a minute, everybody. What if I sort of start at the top and try to tell you everything that happened? Does that sound okay?" I pleaded with them.

Reluctantly they agreed and quieted down. With a great deal of difficulty, I attempted to cover the nearly three months that I had been away from home. After telling them how I had learned to swim (none of them could swim yet), and about going fishing and camping, I finally concluded with the rescue of Jap Ewings from the mine. There was a lot more to tell, but I had run out of steam. I abruptly stopped talking about my adventures and asked if they wanted to walk over to the gas station. "Come on, I'll buy you each a soda pop and maybe even a Moon Pie with the money I earned working at the Silas Green Show," I volunteered.

Well, you can only imagine how excited they were to hear about my treat. And then, almost in unison they asked, "What's a Silas Green Show?"

So on the way over to my dad's Esso station, I told them all about the minstrel show that had come to Quinnimont and the job I had selling candy and Cracker Jack where I was able to earn two dollars each night.

As we sat on the curb under the big maple tree drinking our sodas and eating our Moon Pies, Billy asked me what I knew about the breakout at the jail and the lynching that had taken place outside of town on the hill.

"You're the boy who was the witness in the window that all the newspapers keep on writing about, aren't you?" he prompted. "I know that you have to be that boy. It had to have been you in the window."

"What do you mean?" I replied

"All the newspapers said that there was some kid who looked out the window that night and saw someone at the jail he recognized. Come on, tell the truth. It was you, wasn't it?" Billy insisted.

The twins echoed, "Yeah, tell us the truth, Charlie."

I felt like I was trapped and I didn't have any choice but to fess up and admit that I had been the witness in the window. "Well, guys, I can't tell you everything, but I will tell you that I was staying at the Franks' house the night of the lynching, and of course you know that they live right across the street from the jail. And I did happen to wake up when I heard some noise and looked out the window just as those poor naked guys were being dragged out of the jailhouse."

I was trying to guard my words very carefully so I didn't reveal anything that I wasn't supposed to tell. "And it was Mr. Franks who called the police to tell them about the breakout."

At that point, I decided that I had told them enough and stated firmly, "The police have ordered me not to say anything more until the trial comes up, so don't ask me any more questions."

"But we're your best buddies, Charlie," Billy pleaded. "Surely, you can tell us what happened."

I wasn't going to say another word. "Sorry, but that's going to have to do for now. My lips are sealed," I answered sternly.

And then I abruptly changed the subject. "Hey guys, why don't we go out to the pond and do some swimming this afternoon?"

"That won't be much fun for the three of us," Mark replied. "You know how to swim now and the rest of us don't."

"So, maybe I can teach you. Besides, I want to see the fort that we started building out by the pond before I left town. You didn't finish it while I was away, did you?" I asked, happy to see that the conversation was now going in a different direction.

"Nope, it's just the same as it was when school ended. We were waiting for you to come back," Billy informed me. "But a swim sounds good to me, I guess. Do you really think that you can teach us how to swim?"

"No problem. All you have to do is just kick your feet and stay on top of the water," I told him. "Let's go on home and get some lunch and meet back here about one o'clock," I said standing to my feet. "Come on, I'll race you to the corner!"

The guys never once again asked me about what I saw out of the window the night of the lynching.

It was near the middle of September, shortly after school started, when I was called to the courthouse to meet with a lawyer representing the state of Virginia. A date had finally been set for the trial and they wanted to talk with me about the testimony that I would be giving. Dad picked me up from school that Friday afternoon and drove me over to the courthouse. I must admit that I was a bit nervous since I had never been inside of the courthouse before. It looked pretty imposing with its big white pillars.

The lawyer's name was Harold Summers and when I met him, I realized that I had seen him several times at church. He seemed like a nice enough fellow and treated me with the same kind of respect that he would give to an adult. Mr. Summers led us over to a table in the corner of his office and asked if we would like something to drink. Since we both refused, Mr. Summers got right down to business.

Talking directly to me, he said, "Charlie, I want you to tell me exactly what you saw when you looked out the window of Mr. and Mrs. Franks' home on that night last June."

So I went over the whole story for the umpteenth time, trying not to leave anything out that might be important. I told him all about hearing the noise, peeking out from under the window shade and seeing the hooded men who were gathered around the jail holding guns. I explained how the men had dragged the three colored boys out of the jail and shoved them into a car. Mr. Summers only stopped me one time and that was just to ask a question about which door they used.

The attorney was especially interested about my identification of the man whose face I had seen when his hood had slipped off.

"Are you absolutely certain about his identity?" Mr. Summers asked.

There had never been any doubt in my mind for even a minute about who it was I had seen that night. "It was definitely Alvin Billows," I stated positively. "I had seen him riding around town on his red motorcycle many times. And he even had the name "Alvin" in big letters on the back of his leather jacket. I know what I saw and who I saw. It was Alvin Billows."

Mr. Summers made a few notes on his pad of paper and prompted me to go on with my testimony.

There really wasn't much more to add. I continued to tell him everything that I had observed that fateful night and finally I stopped speaking. "I think I've covered just about everything I saw. There's not too much more to say."

I could tell by his smile that the lawyer was very pleased. He reached out and patted me gently on the shoulder. "You've done great today. Just answer all the questions at the trial to the best of your ability and you'll do fine when you appear in court."

My father seemed to be surprised that I was going to actually be called to the stand to testify before the judge and jury at the trial.

"Is Charlie really going to have to testify publicly in court?" Dad inquired. "Somehow I thought because of his age that he would just have to give some sort of statement that would then be read at the trial."

"Charlie is our star witness of what happened that night at the jail and is our only lead to any of the men who were involved in the lynching. His testimony is vital to the case," the attorney stated.

Mr. Summers then gave us detailed information on the pending trial. "The State has made the decision that because this case is so important and there are so many defendants involved, that it will be necessary to hold several separate trials. The first of these trials will take place in Charlottesville in the District Court and Charlie will be called as a witness. The date that has been selected for the first case to be brought up before the court has been scheduled for Monday, December 8th, 1941."

"But Charlie will be in school then," my father protested.

"I'm sure that he will be excused for a couple of days," the lawyer responded. "Once he has testified, he will be allowed to return home."

After a few more questions, the interview ended. Mr. Summers shook my father's hand and then he reached over and shook my hand too. I felt really grown up when he did that. Only men shake hands.

I was not particularly looking forward to my "day in court," as the lawyer had called it, but of course, as the Lord would have it, my day in court never came.

170

I'm sure that everyone will remember what took place on the day before the scheduled trial. Sunday, December 7th, 1941 was the day when the Japanese attacked Pearl Harbor and World War II was underway. December 7th was described by President Franklin D. Roosevelt as "a date which will live in infamy." Overnight everything changed. Men were donning uniforms and going off to fight for our country and small flags began to appear in the windows of homes designating that a member of the family was serving in the military.

The various trials where I was supposed to testify were put on indefinite hold until further notice. Everyone was involved in the war effort and normal life seemed to be a thing of the past.

It was probably several months later when the judge in charge of the case offered an option to the fifteen men who were awaiting trial for their involvement in the lynching that had taken place the previous June. They could avoid trial, and most likely long prison sentences, if they would voluntarily enlist in the United States Army for the duration of the war. Without exception, they all took the opportunity to serve their country rather than to serve a prison sentence.

As for Jasper Jenkins, he did eventually go on trial where he pleaded guilty to the murder of the three men and to leading an armed rebellion against the state. Jasper was sentenced to life in the state penitentiary, however he only served four years before he was found stabbed to death in his cell. No one was ever convicted of his murder.

Alvin Billows never recovered from his severe injuries nor stood trial for his offences. He was remanded by the judge into the custody of his mother and lived out the rest of his life as an invalid. Alvin died six years later of complications from his accident.

I lived on in Lee's Junction, joining the Cub Scouts and participating in numerous scrap metal and paper drives. I also wrote letters to some of the local boys who had joined the army and navy. Every Saturday I would go to the movies and watch the newsreel clips of the action taking place in both Europe and the Pacific. I sometimes hoped that perhaps the war would last long enough for me to enlist, but deep down inside I wanted it to end immediately so all the killing would stop.

I'll never forget the day when the news arrived that Japan had surrendered after some sort of big bomb was dropped on a couple of their major cities. The war was finally over and the town of Lee's Junction erupted with joy at the news. Bonfires were lit right in the middle of town as everyone celebrated. I had never seen anything like it. Our boys in service would be coming home soon and life would return to normal.

One day when I was nearly fourteen, I went to visit Alvin Billows. I remembered him as a robust young man who always seemed to be full of life. In my mind I still pictured him as the guy riding around town on his red motorcycle. But when Mrs. Billows showed me into his dingy bedroom, what I found was the shell of a man. Alvin was just skin and bones and his hair had turned white, even though he was probably no more than twenty-five years or twenty-six years old.

I walked over to his bed and introduced myself to Alvin, but he seemed to have no idea of who I was. Finally I said, "I'm the boy who was in the window on the night of the lynching."

He looked at me very closely. "You are? But you sure done growed up since I seen you last."

I pulled a chair over to the bed and sat down next to him. "Well, I guess I have grown a lot since the last time you saw me," I agreed. "It's been a pretty long time now. Anyway, I started wondering what had become of you and so I asked around town. When I learned you were right here at your mother's house, I decided to come by and see you."

Hesitating a moment, I added, "I wanted you to know that I've prayed for you a lot since you had the accident. I was there that day when they loaded you into the ambulance."

Alvin seemed stunned when he heard that. "You prayed for me?"

"I sure did. Maybe not every day, but you'd be surprised how often I still think about you and say a prayer." I assured him.

We sat in silence for a few minutes while Alvin seemed to be digesting what I had just told him.

Finally he asked, "Do you realize why I came to Quinnimont that summer you were staying there?"

I nodded my head and answered, "To find me, I guess."

"Yeah, that's right," Alvin replied. "I came not only to find you, but also to kill you so you couldn't identify me. I really thought that I had killed you, and it wasn't 'til I came out of that there coma that I learnt that my bullet had missed you."

I didn't know what to say, so I didn't say anything.

In a minute Alvin spoke again, "But you really prayed for me, even after I took a shot at you?"

"That's right. And last night when I was praying for you, the Lord Jesus told me that you really needed some special prayer right now."

Alvin seemed taken aback. "Are you telling me that Jesus told you to pray for me? For me, Alvin Billows, the guy who tried to kill you?"

"Yes, He really did. You may not know it, but Jesus loves you,"

Alvin kind of laughed a little. "Jesus loves me? Why I ain't never even been to church. The only time I ever prayed was that night in the hospital with that preacher man. You know, I done forgot his name. But I did pray that night and asked Jesus to forgive me."

Somehow I knew that what I was saying was getting through to Alvin. "Jesus did forgive you that night. You may have forgotten about Him, but Jesus has never forgotten about you."

And then I spoke the words that I had really come to say, "And I want you to know – I forgive you too."

I could see tears beginning to form in Alvin's eyes as he listened to my words. He looked over at me and said, "I'm really glad I missed you that night. You seem like a mighty nice young fellow. Thanks so much for coming to see me. Maybe you'll even come back again sometime."

The tears were still on his cheeks, but a smile was on his lips. "I feel so much better knowing that I done been forgiven, not only by Jesus but also by the kid in the window."

I left there that day feeling pretty good about my visit with Alvin and decided that I would drop by to see him every month or so. But it was just a couple of weeks later that I heard he had died peacefully in his sleep.

I asked Dad if I could go to Alvin's funeral and he said he thought that would be nice. He even asked if he could go with me.

The graveside service was held in the back corner of the local cemetery. There were only three people there to watch the coffin be lowered into the ground: Alvin's mother, my dad and me. Oh yes, the undertaker was there too, but he really didn't count because he was just doing his job.

As we stood silently by the grave, Alvin's mother asked if anyone wanted to pray. My Dad didn't respond, so I asked her if she would like me to pray. She smiled and said, "I believe Alvin would really like that. He always seemed a lot happier after that day you came by to visit him."

As I started to pray, I had to choke back tears because I suddenly realized that there was someone else at Alvin's funeral. Jesus was there. He had come to take Alvin home.

Many years have passed now since I stood by the graveside and watched Alvin laid to rest. As I look back through the window of time, I realize what a turning point in my life that childhood summer actually was. Perhaps I should call it a "coming of age" when I put away childish things and began to view the world from a whole new perspective. It was the loss of innocence and a big step into the reality of revenge, prejudice and hatred in the hearts of men.

My family continued to reside in Lee's Junction. The gas station prospered and after the war ended my father acquired five more stations in the area. As a teenager I worked pumping gas and cleaning windshields and my brother Bobby eventually became a partner with my father in the family business.

After high school I went on to college receiving degrees in criminal justice and law enforcement. Upon my graduation I enrolled in the Virginia Police Academy. Perhaps it was riding around in police cars and my association with so many police officers as a youngster that influenced my decision to devote my life to crime detection and prevention. I served as a detective with the Virginia State Police working out of the Richmond office for thirty-five years before taking my retirement.

I married my high school sweetheart, Irene, while I was still in college and would you believe that we had four boys over the next fourteen years. We named them Ralph, Roger, Robert and Randy. It just happened that way. I really wasn't thinking of the four Billows brothers when the alliterative names were picked. I taught my boys how to fish and camp. It's interesting that they all have an almost phobic fear of snakes. The boys are married now and have given me six grandchildren: four boys and finally two girls. I'm really proud of my wonderful family.

My grandparents passed away many years ago, as did the town of Quinnimont. The company store and post office closed down and the inhabitants of the town gradually drifted away to greener pastures.

Sometimes on the way to visit my son, Robert, I drive through Lee's Junction and stop by the cemetery to visit Alvin's grave. And standing there, I look back through the years and remember the time in my childhood when I came to be known as the witness in the window.

NOTES

"The Witness in the Window" is a work of fiction. The characters and many of the places and events mentioned in the book have been birthed directly from the author's mind. However, it must also be confessed that more than a few of Charlie's adventures are based upon real experiences from the life of Jack Coleman as he was growing up.

The lynching incident described in the early chapter of the book can be very loosely identified with an actual event that occurred in Lewisburg, West Virginia, the author's hometown, in December of 1931.

Jack Coleman did indeed visit his grandparents several times during the summer months in the quaint mountain town of Quinnimont, West Virginia as a youngster. Unfortunately, today the town is no longer officially recognized as a viable community. In the year of 1997 the post office was permanently closed and Quinnimont became what is commonly referred to as a ghost town.

Special acknowledgement is given to the author's brother, Jim Coleman, for providing extensive information on the village of Quinnimont. The factual reading material he gathered gave substance to the author's childhood memories and sparked his imagination to make the West Virginia town as authentic as possible.

JACK COLEMAN has pursued many careers in his lifetime. Born and raised in the picturesque town of Lewisburg, West Virginia, he studied at Greenbrier Military School and the University of West Virginia. Upon completing his education, Jack enlisted in the United States Army and served for three years in military intelligence. When his tour of duty in Germany ended, he exchanged his uniform to work as a civilian in the intelligence field for an additional twenty years, including four years in Australia. Jack then retired from government service to go into the service of the Lord. He and his wife founded a large non-denominational church in Laurel, Maryland and pastored The Tabernacle for the following twenty years. The church became recognized around the world as an International Christian Center and the international leadership conferences that were held there attracted delegates from many nations. Recognizing the call upon their lives to world missions, Jack and Jean resigned from the church and began traveling internationally, preaching the gospel on every continent. They currently take several trips abroad every year sharing in churches, Bible schools and conferences. Their hearts have been particularly joined to the nations of India, Peru and Niger. Jack now resides with his wife in Knoxville, Tennessee where he has added the title of author to his career resume. His first novel "Remembering Redbank" is currently available in both paperback and digital copies.

Made in the USA
Charleston, SC
01 October 2013